W9-BMO-596

Harvey
Holds
His *Own*

Praise for *Harvey Comes Home*

"[T]his gently paced, character-driven narrative captivates on every level, transforming a 'lost dog' story into a deeper reading experience. Present-day and historical time lines (with a few grim moments) are seamlessly interwoven and keep readers invested. Back matter reveals that the tale was inspired by Nelson's (*Finding Hope*) grandfather, accounting for the book's authentic, intimate feel. Nelson's first middle grade novel is heartwarming and inspirational; a first purchase."—*School Library Journal* ✱ **Starred Review**

"Throughout, alternating third-person chapters from Maggie, Harvey, and Austin give readers a rounded view of each prominent character....Dog lovers will drool over this multi-generational story."—*Booklist*

"Affecting, riveting, and evocative, this character-driven tale within a tale... believably reveals the best and sometimes the worst of human nature....Much more than a lost-dog story."—*Kirkus Reviews*

"*Harvey Comes Home* is a gentle story about a slow build to friendship between generations that would be of interest to all readers and a wonderful choice for reading aloud. *Harvey Comes Home* is about so much more than a lost dog, and I can see this book being one that any reader would treasure. **Highly Recommended.**"—*CM Magazine*

"Colleen Nelson has written a new book that will especially resonate with pet lovers....Mid-grade readers will enjoy this story of love, loyalty and endurance, in which Tara Anderson shows her versatility by supplying charming black-and-white illustrations."—*Winnipeg Free Press*

"In her first middle-grade novel, [Colleen Nelson] is able to grab the reader's heartstrings while blending a dog story with an intergenerational relationship and embedding profound reflections on the Depression and the Dust Bowl. It's a complete package as Harvey's, Maggie's and Austin's stories converge, integrated with heart and important messages about connecting with others and forgiveness for mistakes made when scared, hurt or alone."—*CanLit for LittleCanadians*

Harvey
Holds
His *Own*

by **COLLEEN NELSON**
Illustrations by Tara Anderson

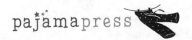

First published in Canada and the United States in 2020

Text copyright © 2020 Colleen Nelson

Illustration copyright © 2020 Tara Anderson

This edition copyright © 2020 Pajama Press Inc.

This is a first edition.

10 9 8 7 6 5 4 3 2 1

www.pajamapress.ca   info@pajamapress.ca

 Canada Council   Conseil des arts
for the Arts   du Canada

 ONTARIO ARTS COUNCIL
CONSEIL DES ARTS DE L'ONTARIO
an Ontario government agency
un organisme du gouvernement de l'Ontario

Canadä

The publisher gratefully acknowledges the support of the Canada Council for the Arts and the Ontario Arts Council for its publishing program. We acknowledge the financial support of the Government of Canada through the Canada Book Fund (CBF) for our publishing activities.

Library and Archives Canada Cataloguing in Publication

Title: Harvey holds his own / by Colleen Nelson ; illustrations by Tara Anderson.
Names: Nelson, Colleen, author. | Anderson, Tara, illustrator.
Identifiers: Canadiana 20200157981 | ISBN 9781772781144 (hardcover)
Classification: LCC PS8627.E555 H375 2020 | DDC jC813/.6—dc23

Publisher Cataloging-in-Publication Data (U.S.)

Names: Nelson, Colleen, author. | Anderson, Tara, illustrator.
Title: Harvey Holds His Own / by Colleen Nelson, illustrations by Tara Anderson.
Description: Toronto, Ontario Canada : Pajama Press, 2020. | Summary: "A plucky West Highland Terrier named Harvey is determined to protect his yard from an intruding animal. Meanwhile, Harvey's owner Maggie struggles to fit in at school, his friend Austin works to prevent his grandfather from losing his job at a retirement home, and new retirement home resident Josephine Fradette clings to her fierce individuality in the face of conformity. Finally, all characters both human and dog find resolution by standing up to adversity"— Provided by publisher.

Identifiers: ISBN 978-1-77278-114-4 (hardback)

Subjects: LCSH: West Highland white terrier -- Juvenile fiction. | Families -- Juvenile fiction. | Old age – Juvenile fiction. | Self-confidence – Juvenile fiction. | Individual differences – Juvenile fiction. | BISAC: JUVENILE FICTION / Animals / Dogs. | JUVENILE FICTION / Social Themes / Adolescence.

Classification: LCC PZ7.N457Ha |DDC [F] – dc23

Original art created with graphite pencil on Canson drawing paper
Interior illustrations—Tara Anderson
Cover design—Rebecca Bender
Text design—Lorena Gonzalez Guillen
Cover image: Oscar, running fast © Christopher Walker

Manufactured by Marquis
Printed in Canada

Pajama Press Inc.
181 Carlaw Ave. Suite 251 Toronto, Ontario Canada, M4M 2S1

Distributed in Canada by UTP Distribution
5201 Dufferin Street Toronto, Ontario Canada, M3H 5T8

Distributed in the U.S. by Ingram Publisher Services
1 Ingram Blvd. La Vergne, TN 37086, USA

For *Ann Featherstone*
–C.N.

For *Buffy*
–T.A.

Chapter 1

Harvey

Early-morning walks are Harvey's favorite. Even better is after a rain when the concrete is cool and damp on his paws. Lampposts and fire hydrants explode with bright, fresh smells, ready for his inspection. He trots from tree to tree, leading Maggie. There's a particularly pungent smell stretching along the curb. Harvey can almost taste it. He tugs, desperate to sniff out the source. "Harvey!" Maggie plants her feet, refusing to move until Harvey calms. Harvey obeys, but only until he feels some give in the leash. Then he is off again, his nose pressed firmly to the ground.

West Highland Terriers are known for their keen sense of smell and their determination. Harvey's hard work is rewarded when his nose leads him to a bag of trash that has been ripped open. Mounds of soggy garbage have spilled out. As much as Harvey would like to stay and investigate every piece, cataloging the smells in his brain, Maggie's voice is sharp with irritation. "Ew, Harvey! Gross! Raccoons did that."

Maggie drags Harvey away, but not before he catches a whiff of the animal's dank fur. The smell sends shivers up Harvey's nose and his tail and ears perk up.

How he hates to leave! The scent could be tracked, its origin discovered. Harvey is a ratter, and his instincts tell him to do just that. He looks back once, longingly. Maggie bends down and scratches the spot between Harvey's ears. "Come on, Harvs. I have school. We have to get home." Instantly distracted, Harvey forgets the strange new odor and trots beside Maggie as they round the corner for home. But somewhere out there is an unfamiliar creature and its scent is now firmly etched in Harvey's memory.

Chapter 2

Maggie

Maggie pulls on the itchy knee socks, part of her uniform for St. Ambrose Academy. She'd been excited about the uniform when she first started. She thought the girls who went to St. Ambrose looked so smart in their kilts, white blouses, and navy cardigans. After a month of wearing the uncomfortable clothing, her enthusiasm has waned.

Starting seventh grade at St. Ambrose has meant lots of big changes for Maggie. The school is farther from home, so she has to leave early in the morning. Her father drops her off on his way to work. She's also learned how to take the city bus home, which has shown her a whole new side of the city. Luckily, her best friends, Brianne and Lexi, also got into St. Ambrose and the three of them are on the bus together. St. Ambrose is where her mother went, and from a young age, Maggie hoped she'd go there too.

There's more homework, and no boys, which Maggie minds more than she thought she would. Not because she particularly liked any of the boys at her old school, but the energy in the room is different without them. It's been a month of getting used to new things and Maggie is glad she has Harvey to come home to.

Nothing makes her happier than to put her key in the lock on her front door and hear Harvey skittering across the tile floor of the front entrance to greet her.

Of course, she'd learned last fall what it meant to lose Harvey. It hadn't been her fault; she'd been on holiday with her family when Harvey had run off. Maggie still isn't sure if it was fortunate or not that he'd been found by Austin, a boy who volunteered at Brayside Retirement Villa. Austin and his grandpa had taken good care of Harvey, but he'd done nothing to help Harvey find his real home and for that, Maggie can never forgive Austin.

If nothing else, losing Harvey proved to Maggie just how precious he is to her.

Chapter 3

Austin

As soon as I step onto the red rug on the sidewalk, the glass doors of Brayside Retirement Villa whoosh open. It's after school and as usual I feel kind of scruffy compared to the fancy entrance. With its wood-paneled walls and huge brick fireplace, wingback chairs, and tables with curly legs, the furniture here is way nicer than anything in my apartment. Grandpa says Brayside has a reputation as the best seniors' home in the city. There's a long list of people who want to move in.

"Hi, Austin." Mary Rose is at the nurse's station beside the front desk. She hands me a newspaper folded so today's crossword puzzle faces out. She doesn't need to tell me it's from Mr. Santos. "Clue 32 Down had him pacing the hall for half an hour."

I read the clue: *Take the* L *in this game.* "*Fortnite*," I say right away, naming the popular online game.

Mary Rose shakes her head and throws up her hands in disbelief. "How would he ever know that?" she mumbles to herself.

"Is Grandpa around?" I ask.

"He's in the basement, I think."

Grandpa is the head custodian for Brayside and has been for seventeen years. I don't know what they'd do without him. He knows every inch of this place and all the residents. I come here almost every day after school to help out. It started last year as a way for him to keep an eye on me. At first, I didn't like it. The old people talked so much and moved so slowly; I just wanted to do my chores and go home.

But then Mrs. O'Brien started baking me her blueberry muffins, the kind with crumble on top.

And Mr. Santos declared me a crossword-puzzle genius. And I met Mr. Pickering.

Just the thought of him makes my throat get tight. Mr. Pickering's death, and all the things I learned from him about his life on the farm, his dog General, and his best friend, Bertie, haven't left me. I still hear his voice sometimes when I'm dusting baseboards outside the suite that used to be his.

Weird to think how close we got in only a few weeks. It was all because of Harvey, this West Highland Terrier I found. If Harvey hadn't come along when he did, Mr. Pickering would never have talked to me. His whole life story would have stayed a mystery.

I miss Harvey almost as much as I miss Mr. Pickering. I know he's with his owner, Maggie, but I still wonder how he's doing and if he ever thinks about me, the kid who took him in for a few weeks last year.

Chapter 4

Maggie

Maggie looks at the form on the desk in front of her. Twenty volunteer hours have to be completed by winter break. She silently groans. On top of all her homework and piano lessons, how is she supposed to squeeze this in too? She can imagine her mom's resigned sigh as she looks at the wall calendar. Almost every square is filled in with appointments and activities for Maggie or her little sisters.

"Does babysitting my brother count?" a girl asks Mrs. Weston.

The teacher shakes her head. "No. There's a list on the back of places we'd prefer you go."

Maggie turns the sheet over. Soup kitchens, food banks, hospitals, and churches. None of them sound interesting to her.

"What about the Humane Society?" another girl asks.

Maggie perks up. Working with animals would be fun. "Unfortunately, you have to be sixteen to volunteer at the Humane Society," Mrs. Weston says. Maggie runs her finger down the list again. That's when she notices a place third from the bottom. To most of the girls, it wouldn't mean anything, but as soon as Maggie sees it, her skin prickles with recognition.

Brayside Retirement Villa.

Mrs. Weston goes through the attendance list, asking the girls where they might like to volunteer. "You don't have to commit to anything yet, but we don't want everyone choosing the same place," Mrs. Weston explains.

Maggie jiggles her foot, thinking. Could she do it? Could she go back to Brayside?

"Maggie?" Mrs. Weston calls.

She hesitates for a moment and then says, "I don't know yet."

She's worried being at Brayside will bring back too many memories of losing Harvey. Maggie adjusts her ponytail and looks around the classroom. Lexi has turned in her seat to whisper to Brianne. More girls make their selections. Maggie worries she'll be stuck with a place she has no interest in. At least she knows Brayside and even though it's filled with old people, it seemed like a nice place. Her foot jiggles under the table with indecision.

She told Austin she'd bring Harvey back to visit but she never has. Maybe seeing Brayside on the volunteer list is a sign.

"Mrs. Weston," Maggie says, raising her hand. "I know where I want to volunteer." Mrs. Weston waits, her pencil poised above the paper. "Brayside Retirement Villa."

Chapter 5

Harvey

Most days, Harvey waits on a chair in front of the living room window for his Maggie to return. As soon as he catches sight of her walking up the driveway, he races from the living room to the front door. It's all he can do not to yip with joy when he hears her key fitting into the lock. Ears pressed flat against his head, his tail wags at Maggie's arrival.

"Hey, Harvey," Maggie says, crouching down. She dumps her backpack on the floor, rubbing behind his ears and pulling him toward her. Harvey licks her cheek, jumping on his hind legs to get into every nook and crevice of her face. Sometimes, Maggie falls back laughing and he can tackle her with more kisses. Today, though, she stands up right away and goes into the kitchen. Harvey pauses to sniff her bag, taking in all the scents she has dragged home from school. Some are familiar, but others he needs to inspect more fully. Her shoes also hold answers to her earlier whereabouts. They taste delicious and even though he knows he's not supposed to, he picks one up and sneaks to a spot behind a chair where he can gnaw on it.

From where Harvey is hiding with the shoe, he can hear Maggie's voice. "You need to sign this," Maggie says to her mother. "It's about doing volunteer hours for school."

Harvey hears the fridge open. Normally he would investigate, but he doesn't want to abandon the tasty shoe, so he stays where he is.

"I'm going to go to Brayside."

"Brayside?" Maggie's mom repeats. "Where we found Harvey?"

Harvey raises his head at the sound of his name, expecting to hear it again as an order to give up the shoe.

"Yeah. I thought maybe I could bring Harvey back to see the old people."

"Your teacher said bringing Harvey was okay?"

"She said I would have to ask Brayside. Some lady named"— Maggie tilts her head to see the name on the sheet—"Mary Rose Aguilar. I'm going to call now," Maggie says. Harvey hears Maggie departing. He stands up with the shoe in his mouth. He hasn't done any real damage to it yet, but he knows it will be ripped away if anyone sees it. He makes a dash through the family room and across the slippery floor of the kitchen, hot on Maggie's heels. If he can get under her bed before she reaches her room, he'll have a few more precious moments to chew on the shoe. Unfortunately for Harvey, but not for the shoe, he underestimated its size. It drags under his belly, slowing him down.

"Harvey!" Maggie says, and catches his collar. "Drop it!"

Reluctantly, he unclamps his teeth and the shoe drops to the carpet. He hangs his head. Caught, once again.

"Good boy," Maggie says, and tosses the shoe back to the front door. "Ew." Maggie wipes her hand on her skirt. "Doggy slobber."

The shoe is quickly forgotten as Harvey follows Maggie into her room and jumps on her bed. Maggie sits at her desk with her cell phone in her hand.

Harvey doesn't know who she is calling or why, but he does pick up on the change in her mood and the tone of her voice.

He sits with his head high, ears pricked with concern. She looks over her shoulder at him and gives a reassuring smile. Only then does Harvey settle on the bed, content to be with his Maggie.

Chapter 6

Austin

When I get to Brayside on Wednesday, Artie is waiting for the elevator. He's got a pile of blankets in his arms. "What's going on?" I ask.

"Mr. Stephens is moving up to the second floor."

Mr. Stephens was in Mr. Pickering's old room. "He wasn't here for very long," I say. It's kind of sad to see someone move up to the second floor. It means they can't live independently anymore.

"That's what happens sometimes. They go downhill fast." Artie drops his voice as Mrs. Luzzi walks by. "And others are here for years."

Like Mr. Pickering. Grandpa told me that he lived in his suite for over twenty years. "Do you know who's moving in?"

"I don't, but Mary Rose does. She was talking to Charlie about it earlier." Charlie is the manager of Brayside. Even though he is technically the boss, it is Grandpa and Mary Rose who really run the place. If there is a problem, they usually deal with it before it gets to Charlie.

The elevator bell dings as the doors open. "Need help?" I ask Artie.

He shakes his head. "This is the last load."

I can't help walking past Mr. Pickering's old room. No matter who lives in it, I'll always think of it as his apartment. It's been emptied out and because Mr. Stephens was there for such a short time, the furniture barely made indents on the carpet.

This is where his recliner was, I think. *And the couch went here.* In the empty apartment, I can almost hear his voice. Stupid to miss someone I only knew a few weeks, but as Grandpa says, it's not how long you know someone, but how well.

"Thought I might find you here," Grandpa says from the doorway. He's got a can of paint in one hand and a ladder in the other.

"I heard about Mr. Stephens," I say. Seeing how quickly some of the old people's lives change makes me sad, but also grateful for Grandpa. He might be in his sixties, but you'd never know it. I can't imagine him living in a place like Brayside, as nice as it is. It just isn't his style. He's lived in the same apartment for ages. It's kind of cramped with furniture and stuff, but he likes it. My mom's always on him to clean it up, but he tells her to mind her own business.

"There's not much to do in this place to get it ready," he

says. "A few touch-ups with paint and a deep clean and it'll be good to go."

"Who's moving in?" I ask.

"A lady. Mrs. Josephine Fradette."

I don't have time to ask Grandpa anything else because we're interrupted by Mary Rose. "I just got off the phone with a girl who wants to volunteer at Brayside." She fixes me with what Grandpa calls "a Mary Rose look," like I should be able to read her mind.

"Her name is Maggie." Mary Rose looks me square in the eye and lets the meaning sink in. "She asked if she could bring her dog with her."

I don't need her to say anything else because now I know why she has that look on her face. Harvey is coming back

Chapter 7

Maggie

Maggie hops out of the car just before eleven o'clock on Saturday and straightens her kilt. Even though it's the weekend, Maggie is representing St. Ambrose, so she had to put on her itchy socks, stiff white blouse, kilt, and cardigan.

"Pick you up at one o'clock," Maggie's mom says. The building is classier than Maggie remembers it. There's a red carpet out front with *Brayside* written in gold, scrolling letters. A striped awning hangs over the sidewalk. The two big planters sitting one on either side of the door are filled with fall flowers. The glass doors slide open, revealing a foyer that reminds her of a fancy hotel.

When Maggie gets inside, she pauses for a moment taking in the space. She'd imagined it smelling like mothballs or cough drops, but detects neither of these things. Good smells come from the dining room and there's a hint of lemon cleaner in the air. Past the reception area, and to the right of the entrance, is a large desk. An engraved gold sign reads NURSES STATION. A woman in a pale pink cardigan looks up and smiles. "You must be Maggie," she says, which puts Maggie at ease. She wipes her hand on her kilt before holding it out to the nurse.

"That's right."

"Mary Rose Aguilar. I'm the head nurse here. We spoke on the phone."

Maggie remembers. Harvey had been staring at her from the bed, as if he knew what was going on. For the first visit, it was decided that Harvey wouldn't come with her. She needed an orientation and could decide how she'd like to spend her time at Brayside. All twenty hours.

Another nurse comes out of the back room. Her name tag says LOUISE. "I remember you," she says. Most people remember Maggie for her auburn hair. It's darkening as she gets older, and hangs down her back in waves. She's got freckles too, which are fading now that summer has come and gone. But Maggie knows it's not her hair that made her memorable to the staff at Brayside. "You're Harvey's owner. Is Harvey here?"

Maggie shakes her head. "Not today. Next time though."

She glances at Mary Rose. "If it's allowed."

Mary Rose winks. "Charlie doesn't know it yet, so keep it to yourself," she whispers to Louise, then she grins again at Maggie.

Maggie's memories of the Brayside nurses are foggy, but she's pleased to see how friendly they are. "Let's start with a tour," Mary Rose says. She is shorter than Maggie, but moves like someone who is used to people following her direction.

Beep beep! Maggie jumps at the sound of a high-pitched horn. Behind her, an old man has come to a stop on a scooter. He is bald, except for a ring of white hair.

"Good day, Mary Rose! Who is this?" he asks.

"Mr. Singh, this is Maggie. She's going to volunteer."

Mr. Singh nods and with a twist of the handle on his scooter zooms back down the hallway. "You have to watch him on that thing," Mary Rose whispers. "He takes the corners pretty fast. And he loves tooting his horn, if you know what I mean."

Maggie smirks, following Mary Rose to the dining room. With its huge chandeliers, it looks like a fancy restaurant. There are fresh flowers on the tables and a whiteboard with today's menu. A few servers bustle around setting tables.

They leave the dining room and pass a bulletin board with a schedule of events. There is everything from chess to yoga to karaoke to knitting. A few more old people wander past them. They all say hello to Mary Rose and give Maggie a friendly smile.

Mary Rose brings Maggie to a dark room at the end of a short hallway. "This is the library," she says, and turns on the lights. The fluorescent bulbs hum as they flicker on. "It doesn't get used much." Maggie can see why. Boxes of books sit on top of tables and the curtains are drawn across the windows. "A resident used to shelve donations and keep it running, but since she moved on…" Mary Rose shrugs as if there is no hope for the space.

Next, they go to the games room. Unlike the library, it is humming with activity. Small groupings of chairs and couches are set up for people to play cards or chat. Two men are playing pool and another group stands at the shuffleboard court at the far end of the room. There's even a Ping-Pong table.

"There's a movie theater too," Mary Rose says. "And the first floor residents' rooms are down the hallway. At the end is the courtyard. Harvey used to love going out there."

"Oh, yes he did!" one of the ladies closest to them says. "We used to watch him from the window."

"He'd chase the squirrels away. Remember that? He'd take off after them like a rocket! A blur of white." A lady with fluffy white hair laughs.

"I miss that little Harvey. He was a sweet dog."

Maggie looks to Mary Rose, who gives her a secretive smile. "Go on. Tell them," she says.

"I'm Harvey's owner." *Real owner*, she's tempted to say. "He'll come with me next time."

"Lovely!" one of the women says. "Austin will be thrilled. He took such good care of him."

Maggie keeps her smile in place, but the words irk her. Austin had no business keeping Harvey the way he did. But she remembers she is here representing St. Ambrose and bites her tongue.

Chapter 8
Austin

All anyone can talk about when I get to Brayside on Monday is Maggie's visit. First, I hear about it from Mrs. O'Brien who met her in the games room. Then, Mr. Singh zips over on his Cobra GT4. "She's bringing Harvey," he tells me.

Harvey's name sits between us. I can't think of Harvey without remembering Mr. Pickering. "I wonder if he'll remember us," I say.

"Harvey will," Mr. Singh says confidently. "Dogs have excellent memories." Down the hall, someone starts playing the piano for the pre-dinner concert. As soon as the dinner music starts, Mr. Singh puts the Cobra GT4 into drive and bolts off. He likes to be first in line.

"Hey, Austin!" Artie claps a hand on my back. "Guess you'll be coming on Saturdays now too? That's when Harvey's coming."

I smile at Artie, but it's not a real smile. The thought of seeing Maggie and Harvey makes me nervous. No one except Maggie and Grandpa knows the truth about how I kept Harvey from finding his home. Instead of taking him to a shelter so they could check for a microchip that would have told them who he belonged to, I'd lied and said his owner couldn't be located. I knew it was wrong when I did it, but I couldn't help myself.

With Harvey at my side I felt special. Mr. Pickering started talking to me. The old people and nurses at Brayside thought I was doing this great thing by looking after a lost dog. Admitting I'd basically stolen him from his owner was the last thing I wanted to do.

But Harvey had found her anyway. Or she'd found him. Harvey was never my dog to keep. I just got to borrow him for a while.

"Austin!" Grandpa barks from down the hall. He's got his toolbox and waves me over. "Give me a hand in here."

Mr. Pickering's old suite is almost ready for the new resident. Grandpa is reattaching the light switch plates and outlet covers now that it's been repainted. He passes me a screwdriver. "Got to get this place ready. Mrs. Fradette is moving in tomorrow." Turns out, there's more to do in here than I thought. Grandpa shows me how to install the closet shelves, reattach the appliances that got moved during cleaning, and how to caulk the shower in the washroom. By the time we're done, it's past my usual quitting time, and Grandpa's too.

We look around the room, satisfied. "Good work, Austin," Grandpa says. "You're a big help."

I shut the door after me, glowing a little from Grandpa's words.

Chapter 9

Maggie

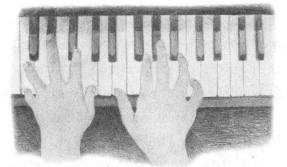

"What did you do on the weekend?" Brianne asks Maggie. The girls are by their lockers waiting for Lexi and for the first bell to ring on Monday morning. St. Ambrose is an imposing, brick building, over a hundred years old. The bells sound like fire alarms and, even after a month, startle Maggie. She expects disaster, not a class change, when they ring.

Maggie waits a beat before answering. Maggie caught the look Lexi gave her in class when she told Mrs. Weston she wanted to volunteer at Brayside. It was an old-people-ewww sort of look, which Maggie had ignored. She wonders if Brianne will react the same way.

"I went to Brayside to start my hours."

Hours may as well be capitalized. The volunteer requirement hangs like an ax over the heads of St. Ambrose students. Most of the girls leave the hours until the end of term and scramble to complete them in the middle of exams.

To Maggie's relief, Brianne doesn't make a comment. "How was it?"

After the tour, Mary Rose had been called away, so Maggie sat down with Mrs. O'Brien and the other ladies in the games room. When one of them mentioned she liked to play cribbage and Maggie said she didn't know how, they decided she needed to learn. Before she knew it, a board and a deck of cards had been pulled off a shelf and they were teaching her.

A little while later, Mr. Singh drove up on his scooter. "Do you play piano?" he asked her.

Maggie nodded. She'd been taking lessons since she was six.

"I knew it!" Mr. Singh fist-pumped the air, like she'd made his day. "Usually, Alma plays a tune, but she's not feeling well today. Why don't you play us something? We always have a little concert before we go in for dinner."

Maggie hesitated. She hated playing in front of an audience.

"It doesn't have to be long. And don't worry if you're out of practice. Most of us are deaf anyway," Mrs. Kowalski, her cribbage partner, said with a laugh.

When Maggie got to the piano, it was five minutes to noon and there were at least fifteen people in the chairs waiting.

Mrs. Kowalski sat down beside a man who must have been her husband. She elbowed him and shouted, "Maggie's going to play," in his ear.

"Who's Maggie?" he asked loudly.

"The girl I was playing crib with."

A tall man with a newspaper folded under his arm and an impressive comb-over walked up to the rows of chairs. "Where's Alma?" he asked.

"She's sick. Maggie's going to play," Mrs. Kowalski said again. "She's a volunteer."

Maggie wiggled her fingers, loosening them up. The old people applauded politely and she gave them a nervous smile. She didn't know what on earth she was going to play.

At the back of the chairs, Mary Rose appeared, pushing an old lady in a wheelchair. Maggie took a deep breath. This piano was a lot nicer than the one she had at home. The keys were cool under her fingertips. She decided to play a song she knew by heart and that she was sure she wouldn't mess up on. When she was done, everyone clapped, but no one got up.

"Play something else," Mr. Singh said. "Alma plays at least three songs."

"Is she any good?" Mr. Kowalski shouted to his wife.

"Yes! Very good!" she yelled back.

Maggie smiled to herself. The old people were a lot less critical than her piano teacher. She played two more songs and when she was done, the applause was more than polite.

"You play beautifully!" Mrs. O'Brien gushed as she moved past Maggie to the line for lunch.

So, in the end, the afternoon had been a lot better than Maggie had hoped for. In fact, she'd sort of enjoyed herself. But Maggie relays none of this to Brianne now. She doesn't want to appear too eager, so instead she says, "It was okay. I'm in charge of organizing the library and next time I'll be able to bring Harvey."

"What if the boy who dognapped him is there?" Brianne asks.

Maggie isn't sure *dognapped* is the right word for what Austin did, but it sounded appropriately dramatic when she relayed the story of Harvey's rescue to her friends last year. "He's only there on weekdays," Maggie explains. She doesn't add that once the old people found out she was Harvey's owner, almost all of them said kind things about Austin and told her how well he had looked after Harvey. Maggie wonders if maybe she judged him too harshly. Maybe Austin the Dognapper deserves a second chance.

Chapter 10

Austin

Whenever we get a new resident, there's a bit of a commotion. The old people are curious and want to know about them. It's like when a new kid starts at school; everyone wants to check them out to see if they have friend potential. But as soon as I meet Mrs. Fradette, I know she's not like any of the other old people at Brayside.

To start with, she still drives. Most people give up their cars when they move into Brayside because it's downtown and there's a Brayside bus that takes them anywhere they want to go. Some of them aren't given a choice because of medical issues. Mr. Kowalski still grumbles about it.

It isn't just that she drives, either. It's *what* she drives. Mrs. Fradette pulls up to Brayside in a car straight out of an old movie. It's so big, it takes up the whole loading zone in front of the entrance. The car is something else. It's red with a band of white on the tail fins. The wheels have white sides and sparkly chrome hubcaps. Grandpa comes up beside me and gives a low whistle. "That's an old Chevy," he says, and shakes his head with appreciation. "Looks like it's in mint condition too."

Mrs. Fradette gets out of the car. She's not much taller than me, which isn't saying much since I'm what Mom calls a "late bloomer." What she's lacking in height, she makes up for in a huge pile of black hair that has to be a wig. A pair of thick black-framed glasses take up half her face, and she's wearing bright red lipstick.

"Yoo-hoo! Young man!" she calls. I don't know if she means Grandpa or me. We look at each other, trying to figure it out.

"Been a while since I was called young," Grandpa mutters, smiling. "Need some help, Mrs. Fradette?"

"I've got my last couple of boxes in there," she says, pointing to the trunk. "Would you mind?"

"Not at all," Grandpa says with a smile. He opens the car door and I sidle up to get a better look at the inside. The front and back seats stretch side to side like benches and are upholstered in red leather; even the steering wheel is red. There's nothing digital, it's all knobs and dials.

"That's a great car," Grandpa says to Mrs. Fradette.

"Chevrolet Bel Air. She's the only car I ever had. I drove her off the lot in 1958 and never needed another one. She's got turbo injection and a V8 engine." Mrs. Fradette pats the hood. "She's been good to me."

Grandpa elbows me: a silent command to get the dolly and move the boxes because she's parked in a loading zone. When I get back inside Brayside, a few of the ladies are at the front doors, watching. "Is that her car, Austin?" Mrs. O'Brien asks.

"Yep."

When I look back, Mrs. Fradette has popped the hood and she's showing Grandpa the engine. Mrs. O'Brien and Miss Lin raise their eyebrows. I'm no expert, but I don't think Mrs. Fradette got the same "How to Grow Old" memo as the rest of them.

Chapter 11
Harvey

Harvey has been in a standoff with a squirrel for the last fifteen minutes. The squirrel came down the fence and had the audacity to race across Harvey's yard. Harvey gave chase and cornered him in a tree. He's been sitting under it, waiting for the squirrel to make its next move.

When he hears Maggie's voice, he is conflicted. He doesn't want to abandon his post under the tree. The squirrel could escape. His concentration is broken by Maggie's voice and a tantalizing offer. "Harvey! Want a treat?"

Possibly the only thing that could pry him away from his post is the promise of a treat. Or maybe a walk. With a final warning bark at the squirrel, Harvey runs to the door. As soon as he takes the treat out of Maggie's hand, he knows something is different. Maggie has a nervous energy about her; it radiates through her fingers. He watches as she puts his treats and a favorite toy into a bag. He's been groomed recently and his undercoat swishes pleasingly as he follows her to the back door.

"We're going somewhere!" she says, and clips his red leash to his matching harness. Harvey jumps up on Maggie's legs. Seeing his leash usually means it is time for a walk. Maggie's mother's shoes tap across the tile floor.

"Car ride, Harvs," Maggie says, leading him to the garage. She opens the door to the car and motions for Harvey to jump in. Harvey hesitates. "Come on," she coaxes. "It's going to be fun."

He obeys because his Maggie has asked him to do it, but he's reluctant. He thought they were going for a walk. She coils the leash on the seat next to him and goes around to the front seat. Once both she and her mother are in front of him, there are clicks and rumbles and the car moves backward. Harvey lies down. All he can see outside the window is sky, and then, as they head downtown, not even that.

Harvey has been this way before, although he doesn't remember exactly when, and the circumstances were very different. Last time, he'd wandered here by himself, lost and afraid. This time, he's got his Maggie with him. The journey that took him days last time takes Maggie's mother only twenty minutes through light Saturday traffic.

But as soon as the car comes to a stop and Maggie opens the door, a burst of scents hits Harvey. They race up through his nose to his brain. He has been here before. This place is familiar.

Chapter 12
Austin

Maggie looks older. Different. I was kind of scared of her when she found Harvey, but that was because I knew I'd been wrong to keep him. I should have tried to find her. A year later, I'm not sure what I'm feeling when I look at her.

She's wearing a uniform and her hair is glossy. I'm in an even grungier outfit than usual because Grandpa said that if I was going to Brayside, I may as well rake the leaves in the courtyard because he didn't get to it on Friday and it's supposed to rain.

Maggie opens the car door and Harvey jumps out. He starts sniffing and it's all I can do not to run over and crouch down with open arms. *He's not your dog*, I remind myself. But man, am I glad to see him.

The nurses at the front desk crowd around me. "He doesn't look any bigger," Mary Rose says.

"Remember how you had to give him a bath?" Artie asks. "He looked like a dirty little rat when you found him."

I remember.

"What's all the commotion?" Mrs. Fradette has only been here a few days and she's become the talk of Brayside. The other residents don't seem to know what to make of her. Don't get me wrong; everyone is friendly to her. Mrs. O'Brien baked her muffins and Mr. Singh made a place for her at his dinner table.

But she doesn't seem like the other old people. In fact, I don't think she *wants* to be like them. She doesn't care if she's doing things differently. I mean, she drives a 1958 Bel Air. To the other residents, this gives her rock star status. Mr. Singh even stopped bragging about his Cobra GT4 around her.

She's still waiting for an answer about why we're all standing around staring outside. "That's Harvey," I say. "He lived here for a while last year and he's come back to visit with his owner, Maggie. He's a therapy dog." *Therapy dog* is a bit of a stretch. Harvey has no special training, but everyone feels good being around him. I mean, look at Mr. Pickering. It was because of Harvey that he told me all his stories.

I don't have a chance to explain anything else before a ball of white fur runs straight at me.

Chapter 13
Maggie

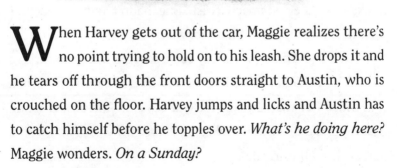

When Harvey gets out of the car, Maggie realizes there's no point trying to hold on to his leash. She drops it and he tears off through the front doors straight to Austin, who is crouched on the floor. Harvey jumps and licks and Austin has to catch himself before he topples over. *What's he doing here?* Maggie wonders. *On a Sunday?*

"He's sure glad to see you," Artie says, leaning down to scratch between Harvey's ears.

A few residents sit on the nearby couches and watch the ruckus. Their faces brighten at the sight of her little Westie. Maggie reaches down to unclip Harvey's leash and stands to the side. Harvey makes his rounds, greeting each person. It's like he knows not to leave anyone out and wants to say hello to all of them. Austin stands up and wipes his eyes. Is he crying? She looks away quickly so she doesn't embarrass him, but she hears the telltale throat clearing and a sniffle.

After Harvey has said hello to everyone sitting, Mrs. O' Brien pats the space beside her on the couch. "Harvey," she calls. "Come here." Harvey runs over and puts his two front paws on the cushion so Mrs. O'Brien can rub his back. She smiles at him like her heart is melting.

"I don't know who's happier—Harvey, or all of us," Mary Rose says with a laugh. From the corner of her eye, Maggie watches Austin. He's not calling for Harvey, or doing anything to draw him away from the old people, but the look on his face makes Maggie's stomach twist. She hadn't considered that seeing Harvey might be hard for Austin.

When she'd first got Harvey back, Maggie had been furious that Austin hadn't tried looking for her. Maggie's mom had reminded her that she was lucky a boy like Austin had found Harvey. He'd been well looked after for two weeks and in the end, it had all worked out.

But now, seeing his reaction to Harvey's return, Maggie feels herself softening. "Harvey's excited to be back," she says. Out of the corner of her eye, she watches Austin watching Harvey as he sniffs Mr. Singh's scooter. She knows the look on his face because she gets it every time she comes home to Harvey. "I'm going to spend my volunteer hours organizing the library," Maggie tells Austin. It was what Mary Rose and Maggie had decided after her visit last week. Even though Maggie had enjoyed her time playing cribbage with the ladies, she thought she'd rather spend her eighteen remaining hours doing a productive, quiet job. Organizing the library is right up her alley. "Can I leave him with you?"

Austin blinks at her. "You sure?" he asks.

Maggie nods and looks at Harvey. He's now tugging on Mr. Singh's shoelace. Maggie holds the leash out. Austin takes it and opens his mouth, probably to say thank you, but Maggie shrugs his gratitude away. She hesitates before adding, "I think he's missed you."

Chapter 14

Harvey

Harvey doesn't even notice when Maggie leaves the room. He's too excited by the scents that zip up his nose as he explores. The odor of the furniture, the floor, even the rubber wheels of Mr. Singh's scooter are all familiar.

Mr. Kowalski wears slippers and as soon as Harvey catches a whiff of the salty, musky smell of them, another memory comes to him: a place of comfort and protection. The warmth of a gnarled hand on his back.

"Harvey!" Austin says with a laugh. "Where are you going?"

Harvey has a singular purpose in mind. He needs to find that space. The scents that will lead him to it are faint, almost undetectable, covered with layers of other scents and buried by time.

With his nose flat to the floor, Harvey takes short, quick inhalations. His black nose quivers. He doesn't notice Austin behind him, or the curious chatter of the old people. All he is focused on is finding his way to the place that is a feeling as much as a location.

There! This door, rife with new smells and a perfume that stings his nose, is the one. He paws at it. His tail is poker straight and his ears are pricked.

"He remembers Walt's room," Mrs. O'Brien says quietly, although she doesn't need to. Everyone knows who used to live here.

Austin bends down and puts his face in front of Harvey's. "He's gone, Harvey. He doesn't live here anymore."

Harvey doesn't understand the words, but he hears the pain in Austin's voice. The strain of the words in his throat. He tilts his head at the boy. Behind him there are murmurs. A parade of old people have come with him and now they watch as Harvey yips and sits down to wait patiently for the door to open. For the old man to appear.

And then the door does open, but the person who appears is not the old man with the salty slippers.

Chapter 15

Austin

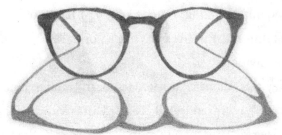

Mrs. Fradette's eyes are magnified by her glasses. She looks at me first, then down at Harvey.

"Do I look like I need a therapy dog?" she asks, blinking. There's a moment of awkwardness from the group of old people standing behind me, but then Mrs. Fradette smiles and it's gone.

"Harvey was quite familiar with Walt, who used to live in this suite," Mrs. O'Brien explains. "I think he wanted to see if he was still here." Harvey picks that moment to stand up and trot past Mrs. Fradette into her suite. He sniffs around her room, checking it out. His leash dangles uselessly in my hand.

"Yep. A regular dog. No manners." But she's grinning when she says it. The cluster of old people in the hallway laugh a little. I don't know if they're laughing at her comment or at Harvey's boldness.

I grab Harvey's harness just before he nudges the door to Mrs. Fradette's bedroom open. I try to guide him away, but he's stubborn and sits back on his legs, refusing to budge. He looks at me like there's been a mistake. *Where's the recliner?* I imagine him thinking. *Or the couch?* I let go of his harness and look him right in the eye. "He's gone, Harvey. He doesn't live here anymore."

Harvey tilts his head at me. He doesn't understand. "Come on, Harvey," I say, and walk toward the hallway, hoping he follows. He starts to, then takes a detour to sniff the legs of the kitchen table. It's in the same place as Mr. Pickering's was, but Mrs. Fradette's is round and has four chairs, instead of only two; spread across it are photos. I guess my eyes linger a moment too long because she comes over and says, "I'm working on my collage. It's harder than I thought."

All the residents at Brayside have collages of photos hanging on the wall outside their suites. It helps us see who they were before they got old. It's a conversation starter too, at least it was with Mr. Pickering. But I've never seen an old person with as many photos to choose from as Mrs. Fradette. There are hundreds, maybe more. Some are in color and some are black-and-white.

"Hard to pick the pictures you want to use?" I ask.

Mrs. Fradette nods. "A whole life can't be contained in one frame. I'd need ten."

"It doesn't have to be your whole life," I say. "Just the most important parts."

She fixes me with a look through those big black-framed glasses. "It's all important."

Harvey decides he's seen and smelled enough and trots back to the hallway. Mrs. O'Brien is still waiting there, but the others have gone to the courtyard. "We're playing bridge at two o'clock today," she says to Mrs. Fradette. "We need a fourth. Do you play?"

Mrs. Fradette winks at her. "Only poker for me."

Like I said, Mrs. Fradette isn't like the other old people. The look on Mrs. O'Brien's face as we go to the courtyard confirms it.

Chapter 16

Maggie

Maggie lugs a box of donated books to a table in the library. She pulls at the flaps and stands back as a burst of musty air hits her. She's been working for almost an hour and hasn't made a dent in the stack of boxes along one wall. But instead of feeling overwhelmed by the momentous task ahead of her, she is invigorated. She doesn't like leaving jobs half done and wants to finish this one before her remaining seventeen hours of volunteer time are up.

This library isn't organized like the one at school. There is no Dewey decimal system. Instead, there are labels on the shelves for BIOGRAPHY, HISTORY, and ROMANCE, and the books are shelved within each section alphabetically by author. So, as Maggie opens the boxes, she reads the back cover of each book and decides which pile she can add it to.

"How's it going in here?" Mary Rose asks. She's got a clipboard in her hands.

"Pretty good," Maggie says. "I'm sorting first, then I'll shelve."

Mary Rose looks at the mess and shakes her head. This is not up her alley at all. She's surprised Maggie was up for the challenge. "Harvey's in the courtyard. If you open the blinds, you can watch him."

Maggie hadn't noticed the window on the far wall. As soon as she pulls open the blinds, sunlight streams in and she realizes what a difference it makes. The library doesn't look half so dreary. The library at St. Ambrose has displays along the tops of the shelves and Maggie thinks that would be a nice addition to Brayside's library as well.

Outside in the courtyard, Austin is tossing a tennis ball to Harvey and the old people are watching and smiling. Maggie can't help grinning. Her little dog is putting on quite a show for everyone. He takes the ball between his front paws and whether it is accidental or by design, he flings it back and Austin catches it. The old people clap as if he's a circus performer. Austin tosses the ball again. It bounces off a wall and Harvey leaps into the air. His short legs don't take him very far off the ground, but he lands with the ball in his mouth to more applause. Austin turns as Harvey races in the other direction after the ball and sees Maggie in the window.

Their eyes lock and neither of them looks away. It could be an awkward moment—in fact, it should be an awkward moment. No one wants to be caught staring at another person, but Austin grins and Maggie smiles too. And she is still smiling when she goes back to unpacking the boxes a few minutes later.

It's not long before Mary Rose comes back and asks for a favor. "Would you mind giving Mrs. Fradette a hand unpacking? I'll think you'll get a kick out of her," Mary Rose adds. "She's quite a character."

Saying someone is *quite a character* is usually another way to say someone is weird. Mary Rose takes Maggie down to the last suite at the end of the long hallway and raps on the door.

A moment later, Maggie is staring at an old lady with a dome of black hair and thick glasses. Maggie's mom would call Mrs. Fradette's look a fashion faux pas, but it makes Maggie smile. *She must really like bright colors*, Maggie thinks. *Or maybe she's color-blind.*

Mary Rose bustles into the suite. "Maggie is volunteering today and is going to help you unpack. Where should she start?"

Mrs. Fradette looks around. "In the kitchen, I guess." The kitchen is really just one bank of cupboards with a microwave, sink, and fridge. Boxes labeled DISHES and POTS AND PANS are stacked on the counter.

"Great! I'll be back in a while." Maggie imagines Mary Rose putting a check mark next to *Help Mrs. Fradette unpack* on her to-do list.

Mrs. Fradette sits down at the kitchen table. Maggie goes straight to the boxes and rips the packing tape off the top. She hopes Mrs. Fradette isn't one of those chatty old people. But Maggie doesn't even have the first layer of packing paper out of the box before Mrs. Fradette asks, "Maggie, is it? Short for Margaret?"

Maggie turns, wincing at the full version of her name. "Yes."

"Don't make that face. Margaret is a good name."

Maggie's never thought so. "It's an old lady na—" She doesn't finish the sentence, but Mrs. Fradette laughs anyway.

"My best friend was Margaret Jane. When we were little, it was always Margaret Jane. But by the time we got to St. Ambrose, she went by MJ."

"St. Ambrose Academy?" Maggie asks.

Mrs. Fradette takes in Maggie's skirt and cardigan. For the first time, she notices the crest over her heart. "Don't tell me!"

"I go there! I'm in seventh grade!"

Mrs. Fradette leans back in her chair. "Seventh grade." She shakes her head. "I never finished seventh grade."

"Why not?"

"It was 1950. All the schools closed early because of the flood."

"All the schools?" Maggie asks doubtfully. "It must have been a bad flood."

"It was. The floodwaters went right up to the doors of the school."

Maggie's eyes widen in surprise. The river is across the street and on the other side of a park. She can't imagine how it could rise up the banks all the way to the school. She wonders if Mrs. Fradette is making this up.

"The whole city shut down. People lost everything. Thousands of people had to evacuate."

"Did you?"

Mrs. Fradette nods. "We went to stay with my mother's family in Laurier, up in northern Manitoba."

"It must have been scary, if you thought you might lose your home."

"I'm sure it was for my parents. For me, going to Laurier was a great adventure. I got to miss school and spend time with my grandpa. We called him Pépère. I didn't want the flood to end! I remember telling my mother as much and she threatened to wash my mouth out with soap for saying such a thing."

Maggie could let the conversation end there. She could go back to unpacking and let Mrs. Fradette sift through the mess of photos on the kitchen table. But when Mrs. Fradette holds up another photo and says, "This is the day we left," Maggie's curiosity takes over and she edges closer to take a peek.

The photo is black-and-white and an unsmiling mother is surrounded by three children. "That's me," Mrs. Fradette says, pointing to the oldest girl. She has dark curly hair parted on the side held in place with a barrette, and she's wearing a coat with buttons. On either side of her are two younger children, a girl and a boy.

"My father tried to keep us in our home as long as he could. A wall of sandbags called a dike had been built to protect our neighborhood but the water kept rising and he got worried. All our neighbors were leaving. My dad, Uncle Wilfred, and Ronny moved all our furniture from the main floor up to the second floor. We didn't have time to pack much, just a suitcase for me and Yvonne and one for my mother. There were so many cousins up in Laurier, my brother, Michel, could borrow their clothes. My aunt Cecile and uncle Joe had eight boys, if you can believe it."

Maggie can't. *Eight* boys?

"Dad drove us to the train station and we said goodbye to him and Ronny. Ronny wouldn't leave. He was a Scout and was helping with flood relief."

Maggie looks more closely at the photo. Behind Mrs. Fradette's family, the train station is packed with people. "Your mom looks stressed," Maggie says.

"She was! I don't think she wanted to leave, to be honest, but it was dangerous to stay." Mrs. Fradette hands Maggie a newspaper clipping. "This is the view from the train."

Maggie stares at the photo. "Whoa. It's like a lake."

Mrs. Fradette nods. "You see? The river flowed right over the tracks. Getting to Laurier usually took four hours by train. It took eight! But it felt like eighty. Mom had packed us sandwiches and there was a family who'd left with just the clothes on their backs sitting near us. I remember Mom shared our food with them."

Maggie hands the newspaper clipping back to Mrs. Fradette. "You must have been relieved to finally get there."

"I suppose so, although my grandparents didn't have the conveniences we had in the city. There was no fridge, just an icebox and a root cellar." Mrs. Fradette makes a face. "We all hated going into that root cellar. Of course, there was no hot water either. There was a pump in the kitchen and we had to boil the well water to get it hot. Bathing was an ordeal and I think Mom just gave up on us ever being clean while we were there. Gave up on me anyways. I was a bit of a troublemaker," Mrs. Fradette says with a wink. "She could control Michel and Yvonne. But I was a handful." Mrs. Fradette leans in with a conspiratorial grin. "My mom was hoping the nuns who taught at St. Ambrose would straighten me out."

"Did they?" Maggie asks, grinning.

Mrs. Fradette throws her head back and laughs. It's a loud guffaw that makes Maggie jump. "Not one bit!"

The knock at the door reminds Maggie that she is supposed to be unpacking, not chatting. She's made no progress on the box of dishes. "I'll get it," she says to Mrs. Fradette.

She's expecting Mary Rose, or one of the other nurses, but it is Austin and Harvey. "Someone's waiting outside for you," Austin says. Harvey weaves in and out of Maggie's legs, his tail wagging as if he hasn't seen her in weeks.

Maggie pulls out her phone. Sure enough, there are multiple texts from her mom and a few phone calls. "I had it on silent," Maggie says. She turns back to Mrs. Fradette. "My mom is here," she says reluctantly. "I have to go."

"Come back again!" Mrs. Fradette says. "Anytime."

The way Mrs. Fradette moves and talks makes Maggie forget that she's at least eighty-three or eighty-four. The dyed black hair helps, but it's not just that. She's still spry, unlike some of the other old people who move slowly because everything hurts. "Sorry I didn't get more done," Maggie apologizes.

"Nonsense. I'm not going anywhere. Neither are my dishes."

Maggie pauses at the door. She thinks she should say something more. Out of the corner of her eye, she sees Austin waiting for her. "Thanks for talking with me," she says.

"Oh, Margaret. No need to thank me for that! One thing I've

got lots of is conversation!" She lets loose another loud burst of laughter.

Maggie realizes that Mary Rose was right when she said Mrs. Fradette was a character

Chapter 17
Austin

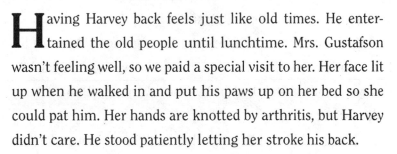

Having Harvey back feels just like old times. He entertained the old people until lunchtime. Mrs. Gustafson wasn't feeling well, so we paid a special visit to her. Her face lit up when he walked in and put his paws up on her bed so she could pat him. Her hands are knotted by arthritis, but Harvey didn't care. He stood patiently letting her stroke his back.

It's funny how a little dog can help people without even trying.

He wasn't allowed in the dining room, so while the old people ate, we sat on the couch in the foyer. He curled into a ball beside me, tired from all the exercise. I rubbed the spot behind his ears that I knew he liked. He closed his eyes and sighed, the way he used to with Mr. Pickering. "You're a good dog, Harvey," I whispered. Just the two of us, and this moment of quiet, made me miss Mr. Pickering even more.

We're still sitting there when I see the SUV that dropped Maggie off pull up to the curb. Mary Rose is at the front desk. "Where's Maggie?" I ask.

"She's with Mrs. Fradette," Mary Rose says.

I raise my eyebrows. Mary Rose catches the look right away.

"Oh, you think you're the only one who's any good with the old people?"

"I'm just surprised," I say.

"Well, no one has left the suite screaming, so I think they're getting along fine."

"Come on, Harvey." I stand up and Harvey follows me down the hallway to Mrs. Fradette's suite.

Mom asked that morning why I was going to Brayside to-day. She smiled when I told her about Harvey coming back to Brayside for a visit, but also gave me a warning. "Don't get any ideas about a dog."

I promised I wouldn't, but she didn't know that ever since we'd taken in Harvey, getting a dog was all I thought about. I knew it would never happen—we couldn't afford one, and our apartment was too small—but it didn't stop me from wanting one. Even though I knew it was wrong, I couldn't help wishing Harvey was mine.

Okay, so I'll admit, when I knock on the door, I really am wondering how things are going with Mrs. Fradette and Maggie. Nothing against Maggie, but she looked a little nervous when she arrived. It made me wonder if she thought Brayside would be an easy place to volunteer because Harvey would be the one doing all the work.

But she's smiling when she opens the door, and so is Mrs. Fradette, who is sitting at the kitchen table behind her. In fact, it looks like they kind of like each other. I guess Mary Rose was right.

Chapter 18

Harvey

That evening, Harvey presses his nose against the cool glass of the sliding door that leads to the backyard and growls. "What's out there?" Maggie asks. She bends down to his level, but can see nothing. The days are getting shorter and the neighbor's fence across the yard is barely visible in the dark. "Do you see a squirrel?"

What Harvey has seen is not a squirrel. It isn't a chipper, mischievous creature that scampers along branches. It is a slinking, stinking animal; a thief and a brute. It is a raccoon. And this particular raccoon is looking for a place to spend the winter.

Unfortunately for Harvey, she has found it.

When Harvey is let out in the morning he can smell it. Something feral and familiar. The air is full of it. He has caught this scent before; it is lodged in his scent memory.

Harvey goes into tracking mode. Tail up. Ears perked. He raises his nose into the air. His hair bristles with curiosity, and something else: determination. Something has invaded his territory and he wants to know what it is.

Harvey moves to the fence and sniffs along the bottom, but there is no scent. Harvey raises his nose. Whatever has been in his yard has been up there, crawling along the top of the fence. Slowly, so as not to lose track of the odor, he moves past trees and plants, until he arrives at the shed in the corner.

Harvey has never been fond of the shed. It is in a dark, shady corner of the yard under a crab apple tree. When the fruit falls to the ground, it sits and rots, filling the air with a sour smell. Inside the shed are roaring, spitting machines; their noises leave Harvey running for cover.

But this morning, Harvey has a job to do. He inches closer to the shed and pauses. The scent is all around him now, not just along the fence. The creature! She has been slinking around and the smell is so strong she could be here now. Harvey approaches cautiously. He barks to alert his Maggie.

It doesn't matter to Harvey that it is barely seven in the morning, or that his barks shatter the neighborhood's quiet.

He is intent on warning Maggie and letting the thing know that it is not welcome in Harvey's yard.

"Harvey!" Maggie's mom whisper-shouts from the deck. "Harvey, be quiet!"

Harvey can't turn around or obey the command. He must continue to bark. It is important that everyone know there has been an intruder. From a few houses over, his barks are echoed by Rosie.

Now two Westies are on the case, followed by Lola, a dog who lives behind them. And farther down the street, Gordie the golden Lab lets out a deep, rough *woof*. They have all heard Harvey's insistent call to action.

"What's going on?" Maggie says, joining her mom on the deck. She's in her pajamas and still rubbing sleep out of her eyes.

"He's going to wake up the whole neighborhood!" Maggie's mom says.

"Harvey!" Maggie calls. "Harvey, come get a treat!" She uses her best cajoling, singsong voice and in a short lull of barking, it reaches Harvey.

"Treat, Harvey," she says again. "Want a treat?"

With a final rumbly bark, he races across the yard and back to his Maggie, who is on her knees on the deck waiting for him. "Good boy, Harvey," she says, rubbing his back.

Harvey's tail wags. He licks Maggie's warm, sleepy-smelling skin and follows her inside. For the moment, the intruder is forgotten. The scent from outside, though, won't be. It will lurk in the back of Harvey's mind until the next time he is outside.

Chapter 19

Maggie

Maggie hadn't intended on thinking about Brayside once she left. But all week, she finds herself thinking about the library, the old people, and especially Mrs. Fradette. "Did you know there was a flood in 1950? The city was evacuated," she says to her friends at lunch on Friday.

Lexi shakes her head. "Did you know I don't care?"

There's a moment of uncomfortable silence at the table. "That was harsh, Lex," Brianne says. Maggie keeps quiet. Lately, she's noticed Lexi gives her attitude about lots of things.

"Well, sorry, but it's just a lame thing to talk about."

"I thought it was interesting," Maggie says. She feels a blush creeping up her cheeks. "Or at least surprising."

Brianne tries to bridge the gap of awkwardness by talking about the movie that opens this weekend; the one the three were excited to see. But her chatter can't undo the damage that's been done and it's a relief when the bell rings for afternoon classes. "What's with Lexi?" Maggie whispers to Brianne as they head to their lockers.

Brianne chips at her turquoise nail polish and shrugs. "I don't know." But Maggie gets the sense that Brianne does know. It bothers her all day and when the dismissal bell rings, she doesn't wait for the girls at their lockers like usual. She goes straight to the bus stop and when the bus arrives, she finds a seat at the back.

Lexi and Brianne get on together. Neither of them looks for her or seems curious about where she might be. She checks her phone, but there are no texts asking where she is. Even though she is on a bus full of people, Maggie has never felt so alone. She slouches lower in the seat because now she doesn't want to be discovered. When the bus comes to her stop, she keeps her head down and slinks out the back door. The argument, or whatever it was, will blow over if she doesn't make a big deal about it.

For the rest of the evening and on Saturday, Maggie tries not to let her friends' behavior bother her, but worry keeps creeping in. Is Lexi still annoyed with her? Should she text her to smooth things over? Her spirits are boosted when she posts a picture of Harvey on Instagram and Lexi and Brianne both like it. Maggie decides she's being too sensitive. Lexi's always had an edge to her, it's just never been directed at Maggie before.

When Maggie wakes up on Sunday morning, she checks the notifications on her phone. There's the usual onslaught of posts from girls she doesn't know well and then there's one from Lexi. It's a photo of two bags of popcorn at a movie theater. One bag is in Lexi's hand and the other is being held by someone with chipped turquoise nail polish. Brianne.

Maggie's heart sinks as she realizes her friends went to the movie without her. She slides down on her bed as Harvey jumps up, ready to play, which is the last thing she wants to do right now.

Lexi posted the picture knowing Maggie would see it. She quickly checks her text messages. Maybe they invited her and she didn't see the text? But there is nothing from Lexi or Brianne since last Thursday. Her mind spins trying to make sense of it. Had they been planning the movie night for days? Or did it happen on the bus ride on Friday? Had she been excluded on purpose, or accidentally? Maggie racks her brain trying to decide what to do. Finally, she sends a text to Brianne.

Is Lexi mad at me?

Three dots appear on her phone and Brianne's reply comes a moment later. *IDK. Why?*

Maggie is too nervous to type her real suspicion: that Lexi wants more popular friends. Girls who hang out with boys and go to parties; girls who are more fun than Maggie. Maggie has seen her watching the popular girls in the cafeteria. She's noticed that Lexi has started wearing makeup and rolling the waistband of her skirt up a few inches so it sits mid-thigh. But instead she types her response to Brianne: *Just wondering*, and then turns her phone off.

Lexi and Brianne are doing exactly what they all swore they'd never do: shutting one person out. At a sleepover at Lexi's house before seventh grade started, they'd all promised they'd stay friends no matter what. It had been Lexi's idea too. Maggie is tempted to send a text reminding the girls of their oath. But then she imagines Lexi mocking her as childish for bringing up the promise, even though it was only six weeks ago. For the first time in her life, Maggie is glimpsing how complicated friendships can be.

Chapter 20

Harvey

Getting up on a bed carrying a tennis ball in his mouth is no small feat for a little Westie. Usually this accomplishment is met with praise. But today, Maggie ignores Harvey and stares at her phone.

Harvey nestles closer to Maggie, nuzzling her leg. He wants to play. He drops his tennis ball beside her, but Maggie doesn't notice. With a sigh, she tosses the phone onto her bed and slouches down. Harvey slides closer. "Oh, Harvs. At least you're still my friend." Maggie takes Harvey's face in her hands and pulls it to her. He licks away her salty tears.

"Maggie, time to go!" her mom calls from downstairs. Maggie wipes her eyes and sits up.

Harvey knows something is wrong. His Maggie is usually bright with movement and chatter; sharp and inquisitive. But today, she rises sluggishly. Harvey tilts his head at her. "Let's go, Harvey," she says. "We're going to Brayside."

Harvey lies down in the back seat, keeping an eye on Maggie, who sits in the front with her mother. It's Maggie's mom who does most of the talking as she drives. Maggie stares out the window, silent and distracted.

When they arrive at Brayside, Harvey sees the flashing lights of an ambulance. "Oh no," Maggie murmurs as Harvey jumps out of the car, curious about the people rushing in and out. A gurney is wheeled past and Harvey moves out of the way of its wheels. All the smells and sounds disorient Harvey. He barks, overwhelmed and alert.

"Shush, Harvey," Maggie says, and yanks his leash. When there is a break in the activity, Maggie leads him through the front doors. Compared to the busyness of the sidewalk, Brayside is decidedly calmer, but Harvey senses agitation when Mary Rose comes around the desk to greet him.

"Who was that?" Maggie asks Mary Rose. Harvey's ears rotate to the siren, blaring again now that the ambulance is headed to the hospital.

"Mr. Stephens," she says, shaking her head. "He just moved to the second floor."

"Is he going to be all right?"

"I don't know. I hope so."

Maggie sighs and Harvey moves closer to her. He knows she needs him, even if he doesn't understand why.

The front doors slide apart and Harvey catches a whiff of boy sweat and stinky sneakers. With a *yip*, he runs as far as the leash will let him go in the direction of the smell. Austin has arrived. Harvey jumps and licks, overjoyed to see him. Austin bends down. "Hey there, Harvey!" Harvey puts his front paws on Austin's thighs and peers into his face. "What is it?"

"Mr. Stephens went to the hospital," Mary Rose says.

"Oh." Austin gently pushes Harvey off his legs and stands up. His voice is heavy now, all the excitement drained away.

"It's good you're here," Mary Rose says to Maggie, but she looks at Harvey. "We can use a little Harvey love."

At the sound of his name, Harvey goes over to Mary Rose. She crouches down. "Can't we?" she says in a high-pitched singsong voice. "Yes, we can." Harvey stays still, enjoying the under-the-collar scratches Mary Rose does so well.

"Rough morning?" Austin asks.

Mary Rose sighs and stands up, back in work mode. "To say the least." She turns to Maggie. "Would you mind going to Mrs. Fradette's room? I was in there yesterday and she's still got boxes all over."

"Sure," Maggie says, and hands Austin the leash. "He probably needs to go out." Harvey bristles at his Maggie's voice.

She's not scared, or sick; he'd smell those things on her, but something is wrong. So, despite the fact that Austin has his leash, when Maggie walks away, Harvey goes with her.

Maggie stops and shakes her head at him. "No, Harvey. You're staying with Austin."

Harvey blinks at her, not understanding. "I'm okay," she says. Her voice is brighter than before. Harvey gives a quick yip. *Are you sure?*

Maggie rubs under his chin. When Austin calls him back, Harvey hesitates for a second, but then obeys.

Chapter 21

Harvey

Smells are organized in Harvey's brain according to frequency. He has an infinite amount of room for them, which is what makes Westies like Harvey excellent ratters. As soon as he and Austin set foot and paw on the sidewalk in front of Brayside, he catches a few familiar scents. There is car exhaust and soggy leaves, and the odor of gritty concrete. But the air is laced with unfamiliar scents too that Harvey does his best to capture.

Austin is patient. He lets Harvey sniff for as long as he wants at lampposts and fire hydrants. The corners of buildings are also rife with odors, as are a few sticky spots on the cement.

Whenever they pass someone, Harvey veers in their direction. Most times, Austin pulls him away before he can say hello.

At each corner, Austin makes Harvey wait until he is sure it is safe to cross. Harvey pokes his nose out, his eyes and ears alert. A new smell, something not cataloged in his brain, catches his attention at an alley entrance. Harvey is desperate to investigate and yanks hard on the leash. "No, Harvey," Austin says.

But Harvey is insistent. He lurches forward, dragging Austin behind him.

"Whoa, Harvey!" Austin says, laughing. "What is it?"

Harvey is so intent on tracking down this new odor that he forgets there is anyone on the other end of the leash.

The alley is dark and narrow. Tall brick buildings block almost all the natural light. Dumpsters overflowing with bags sit on either side. Normally, the dumpster odors would be enough to distract Harvey, but not today. He is drawn to a different smell. His nose hovers just above the pavement. It zigs and zags following the scent.

But dark alleys aren't known for their safety. Austin plants his feet. "Come on, Harvey. That's far enough." Harvey strains and whines. Just a little farther, he begs Austin.

Austin sighs and goes one more step and then he hears something. A whimper.

Chapter 22

Maggie

"**M**argaret!" Mrs. Fradette exclaims when she opens the door. "What a lovely surprise!"

The warm welcome pushes all thoughts of Maggie's friends out of her head. She's surprised how happy she is to be back helping Mrs. Fradette. Her suite, despite its unpacked boxes, feels safe and familiar.

Even though Mary Rose sent Maggie hoping she'd get some work done, Mrs. Fradette is in no rush. She brings Maggie over to the kitchen table where an array of photos is spread out. "I'm trying to choose my favorite," Mrs. Fradette says. She's got about twenty pictures of her car lined up in a row.

Sometimes the car is parked on the street, and sometimes it's in a driveway with a house behind it. There are a couple at the beach and one with mountains in the distance. Mrs. Fradette is in most of them and if Maggie knew more about fashion, she'd know that the beehive hairdo in one is from 1968 and the long denim skirt in another is from 1975.

"I like this one," Maggie says. Mrs. Fradette is leaning against the car and looking off to the side. She's got a patterned scarf tied around her head and is wearing huge sunglasses. "You look like a movie star."

Mrs. Fradette beams at Maggie. "I like that one too. That would have been taken in 1963. I stole that look from Jackie Kennedy. People said I looked like her with my dark hair."

"You've had your car for a long time," Maggie says.

"Since 1958."

Maggie does the math. "Sixty-two years!" she blurts. She's never heard of anyone owning the same car for that long.

Mrs. Fradette nods. "It's going to be hard to let her go."

"You're selling it?"

"My son thinks I should. I don't drive her much anymore and now that I'm here..." Her voice drifts off. "I don't really need it."

As she talks, Maggie can hear the tug in Mrs. Fradette's voice. "You shouldn't sell it until you're ready," Maggie says. She doesn't know if she's allowed to offer advice like that to the old people, but she can't help herself.

Mrs. Fradette raises her eyebrows at Maggie. "Thank you for saying that, Margaret. It's nice to meet a young person with some sense."

Maggie feels her cheeks warm at the compliment. She likes the grateful look Mrs. Fradette gives her, and the way the old lady's lips turn up at the corners.

Chapter 23

Harvey

Harvey sticks his nose behind the pile of garbage bags. They're full of rotten odors, and normally he'd love to rip them open and burrow his snout in all the stink, but at this moment, he barely notices them. There is something alive buried in the trash.

Austin helps, carefully lifting the bags up and away. He can hear a faint sound, almost drowned out by traffic from the street. Harvey pushes in with his nose until he finds a cardboard box. There! Inside is the source of the scent. Beside him, Austin gasps.

Harvey puts his paws on the edge of the box and peers in. Even though it isn't moving, Harvey knows it is alive. But for how much longer? "Poor thing," Austin whispers, crouching beside Harvey. Gently, Harvey nudges it with his nose. The puppy takes a breath.

Harvey's excitement grows. He would like to yip, but something tells him no. A fragile thing like this needs something Harvey can't give.

"We can't leave it here," Austin says, glancing up and down the alley. He drops Harvey's leash and takes off his hoodie. Harvey watches as Austin moves slowly, picking up the pup and wrapping it. The wee thing is so small, only its tiny pink nose pokes out. Austin makes sure it can breathe and shows Harvey. Harvey presses his nose against the newborn and inhales. Under the filth of the alley, he can smell its newness. It's quivering with hunger and fear. Harvey gives it a lick. *You are safe now. This boy will care for you.*

Austin bundles the puppy against him and picks up Harvey's leash. "Let's go, Harvey. We have to bring it back to Brayside."

Harvey walks with quick, efficient steps. He's not interested in sniffing fire hydrants or lampposts. *Out of my way, people,* he says with his trot and his tail. *We have important business. New puppy here!* No one gets in their way. In fact, with Austin following closely, they make it back to Brayside in record time.

As soon as Harvey is inside the sliding doors, Austin drops the leash. "Artie, look!" he says. "Look what Harvey found." Austin kneels on the carpet and puts down the hoodie. Harvey stands beside him, watching. The tiny dog's eyes are closed. A white strip stretches from a pink-nosed snout to the nape of its neck, and its legs are white too. Splotches of light brown surround both eyes and floppy ears, and there's another brown spot on its side.

Artie comes around the front desk and bends down beside Austin. "Harvey found it?"

"In a box in the alley. Right beside a dumpster."

Artie's mouth tightens. "Who would do that?"

Austin sits back on his heels. "What do we do? It's so little. I can't even tell if it's a boy or a girl."

Up until now, Harvey has stayed back, watching. But the pup is shivering. Instinctively, Harvey steps onto the sweat-shirt and circles. Austin gasps. "Harvey! No! You'll hurt it!"

Harvey ignores Austin. Carefully, he positions himself so the puppy's body will be parallel to his and lies down. The puppy nestles closer, seeking Harvey's warmth. This is how Maggie finds him a few minutes later when she comes out of the suite at the end of the hall.

Chapter 24

Maggie

At first, Maggie thinks something has happened to Harvey. Why is he lying down in the middle of the entrance with Austin and Artie crowded around him? Her heart jumps to her throat and she breaks into a run. As she gets closer, she sees he's sitting like a Sphinx guarding an ancient Egyptian tomb. Her steps slow and she exhales with relief. "What's going on?"

"Harvey found a puppy," Austin says. And then Maggie sees it, tucked against Harvey's side. It looks impossibly small.

"What do you mean? Where?"

"In an alley, a few blocks away. He smelled it, I guess. He dragged me in there and then started sniffing through the trash. It was in a box under a bag of garbage."

Maggie leans in. "Is it okay?"

Austin nods. "I think so."

"Awww," Maggie coos. "How old do you think it is?"

"Can't be more than a couple of days," Artie says.

Maggie wilts at the thought of someone tossing out a newborn puppy like a piece of garbage. "What are you going to do? Is there a vet nearby?"

"They'll tell you to take it to the Humane Society or a shelter," Artie says.

As they talk, Harvey puts his head down and curls his body around the puppy. Maggie feels a rush of love for him and reaches out to stroke his back.

In the end, Artie makes some calls and the shelter a few blocks away agrees to take it. "I'll go," Austin says. He knows Artie can't leave work and Maggie's mom will be here any minute to pick her up.

"Do you know where it is?" Maggie asks.

Austin nods. *It's where I should have brought Harvey last year*, he thinks, but doesn't say. He looks at the puppy and wonders if he'll be able to do it, just leave it there. But it's so helpless and small; he has no idea how to care for it.

"My mom could drive you," Maggie offers.

Austin shakes his head. Walking with the puppy cuddled

against his chest will give him a few more minutes with it. "I wish I could keep it." He sighs.

"Why can't you?" Maggie asks, although she suspects what the answer will be.

"There's no way my mom will let me."

Maggie feels a twinge in her chest. If anyone deserves to have a dog, it is Austin. She can practically taste how hard giving up the puppy will be for him. "It's really little," Maggie says, trying to make him feel better. She can't imagine what her mom would do if she came home with a stray newborn. Maggie runs a finger along the puppy's snout. The pink nose wiggles and it looks like the puppy is trying to open its eyes but doesn't have the energy.

Outside, Maggie sees her mom pull up to the curb. She sighs and wishes she didn't have to go. "Come on, Harvey." Maggie stands up, expecting Harvey to do the same, but he stays where he is. "Har-vey," Maggie says. "We have to go."

Harvey doesn't budge.

Maggie knows how he feels; she doesn't want to leave the puppy either. She and Austin exchange a look. Austin reaches down and gently scoops up the puppy. It fits comfortably in his hand and when he holds it against his chest, he can feel its heart beating. Little claws poke out of pink paws, the pads still velvety soft.

Finally, with the puppy safe in Austin's arms, Harvey stands up. "Are you sure you don't want a ride to the shelter?" Maggie asks.

"I think I'll just spend a bit more time with it," Austin says looking down at her. "Make sure it's okay."

Artie shakes his head. He's got the Animal Shelter website open on his phone. "Says here newborns should be brought in right away."

Austin's face falls.

Maggie knows how easy it is to fall in love with a puppy. She felt the same the moment she laid eyes on Harvey. The difference was, she knew she was bringing Harvey to his forever home and not leaving him in a shelter.

Chapter 25

Austin

The shelter is just like I remember it from last year when I tried to bring Harvey. There's a lot of excited barking as soon as I walk in. Dogs in small rooms sleep pressed against the walls. Some of the smaller ones are in cages. They all have food and water and I know the shelter is doing the best it can to look after them, but I still want to get out of there as fast as I can and take the puppy with me. It's just too sad to know all those abandoned dogs need a home.

A woman with a name tag that reads JOANNE takes the puppy away and disappears to the back with it. When she comes back, she asks me where and when I found her. I explain how Harvey sniffed it out in the alley a few blocks away. "Is Harvey your dog?" she asks.

I shake my head. "I was just walking him."

"He's a hero," she says with a smile. "And so are you for bringing this little one in. We'll make sure she's fed and cleaned, and a vet will take a look at her."

"Her?" I ask. "It's a girl?"

Joanne nods. "If she makes it, she'll be ready for adoption in about six weeks."

If?

"We're always looking for good families to adopt or foster our animals. Take a brochure," she says, handing me one from a stack on the counter. I want to tell her I'd adopt every dog in there if I could. If my mom would let me. If we had more money. If we had a bigger apartment. That's a lot of *if*s.

I say goodbye to Joanne and leave the shelter, but now instead of a one-pound puppy, I'm walking away with a hundred pounds of guilt. I assumed Mom would say no to the puppy, but what if I was wrong? What if she saw the puppy and had a change of heart?

Losing Harvey, who was never mine to begin with, was hard. But finding a puppy all alone like that? What if she's my second chance?

Chapter 26

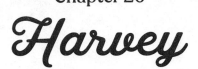

Harvey

That night Harvey jumps onto Maggie's bed. He circles until he finds just the right spot in the crook of her knees. He catches a whiff of the puppy's scent on himself. He gives a loud sigh. "Oh, Harvs," Maggie says, and scoops him up. She wraps one arm around his body and pulls him close to her. With his Maggie's breath warm against the top of his head, and her hand on his belly, Harvey drifts to sleep.

The scent of the puppy is cataloged in his memory. It will get buried deep under other smells, though, because Harvey has no reason to pull it up. After all, he will most likely never see the puppy again.

Chapter 27

Maggie

When Maggie wakes up on Monday morning, her first thought is the puppy Austin found. She thinks about her as she gets her breakfast and as she checks the St. Ambrose online calendar. With a groan, she sees there is a Student Leadership meeting after school today. Maggie signed up for Student Leadership but isn't really interested in it; she only signed up because Lexi had wanted to. After everything that's happened recently with Lexi and Brianne, the thought of spending time with her friends after school turns her stomach into a pretzel.

The problem is Mrs. Weston, who runs the Student Leadership Committee. She was overjoyed that three girls in her homeroom had signed up. Maggie knows that if she bails without a good reason, Mrs. Weston will convince her it's too early in the school year to quit and will drag her back.

Maggie stares at the cereal box, thinking. If she had a good reason not to go to Student Leadership, Mrs. Weston wouldn't push the issue. It occurs to Maggie that squeezing in more volunteer hours at Brayside might be the answer. There's no reason her visits need to be limited to weekends. Brayside is close enough to St. Ambrose that she could easily walk there after school. "Mom, can I go to Brayside today? I'll walk over and Dad can pick me up on his way home from work."

Maggie's mom is in the middle of packing lunches for the twins. The two girls are eating Cheerios in front of the TV and Harvey is sitting beside them hoping for handouts. Her mom shrugs. "Fine with me. I won't be able to drop Harvey off though."

"I know. He's not as integral to the volunteer hours as I thought he'd be. I'm mainly helping Mrs. Fradette unpack." *Or trying to*, Maggie thinks with a grin.

Maggie's mom turns at Maggie's use of the word *integral*. Between her daughter's desire to volunteer and her growing vocabulary, she thinks the St. Ambrose tuition is already proving its worth.

Maggie goes to brush her teeth, relieved that she got out of a committee she didn't want to be on in the first place and surprisingly happy to be going back to Brayside. Old people, at least the ones at Brayside, aren't what she expected.

* * *

When her dad drops her off at school, Maggie steels herself for the walk into the building. Usually, Lexi and Brianne wait at their lockers for her to arrive so they can walk into class together. Maggie prepares herself for the possibility that today they won't be there.

It is a huge relief when she turns the corner and sees the girls leaning against their lockers like usual. The three of them have the normal conversation about how much homework they had and how long they studied for the upcoming math test. The knot in Maggie's stomach loosens. Maybe she was making something out of nothing. It was just a movie, after all.

But then things go downhill at lunch. "We've got Student Leadership after school," Brianne reminds both of them. Lexi nods, licking the last smear of pudding off her spoon. Brianne looks at Maggie. "You're coming, right?"

Maggie hesitates. She is really looking forward to going back to Brayside. She wants to know what happened with the puppy and is determined to get at least one box unpacked for Mrs. Fradette. "I can't. Not today."

"Why not?" Lexi's question comes out more like an accusation. "It's the election today. You have to vote for me for seventh-grade rep."

Maggie fumbles for an answer. "I forgot and made plans."

"Seriously, Maggie." Irritation is plain in Lexi's voice. Maggie tries not to let it get to her, but she can't help wondering if this morning's warm welcome was because they wanted her vote.

"Maybe you can talk to the teacher and vote before you leave?" Brianne suggests.

Maggie says nothing. The snarkier Lexi gets, the less inclined Maggie is to vote for her.

Lexi purses her lips. "Where are you going, anyway?" Maggie knows there is no explanation that will improve the situation, so she tells the truth. "Brayside."

Lexi rolls her eyes. "You and your volunteer hours. It's like an obsession."

Maggie doesn't know how to take Lexi's comments. They sting and she isn't sure if it's what she says or the way she's saying it. She doesn't respond to Lexi, but she also doesn't offer to change her plans. For Maggie, this small act of defiance matters.

Chapter 28
Austin

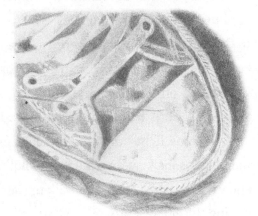

All I can think about is the puppy as I walk to Brayside after school on Monday. Mom shook her head when I told her the puppy would be ready for adoption in six weeks. "We can't look after a dog right now," she said. "I'm sorry, Austin. One day, maybe, but not now."

Knowing a dog of my own was an impossibility didn't stop me from going back to the alley on my way to Brayside after school. The dumpster was empty. The box the puppy had been in and all the other trash had been picked up. I didn't want to think about what would have happened if Harvey hadn't insisted we go down that alley.

"Hey, Austin," Artie says from the front desk when I arrive. "Your grandpa had to step out for a while. But Mr. Kowalski just called. He says he's got a screw loose." Artie grins at his own joke. "Bathroom towel bar," he explains. "Do you mind taking care of it?" Jobs like this one I can do without Grandpa's supervision. "While you're at it, Charlie left a note that he has some burned out light bulbs in his office."

I head to Grandpa's office in the basement. The fluorescent lights flicker to life. Tools are all over; hanging up on a pegboard, in coffee cans on the shelf, and in his big five-drawer tool chest. I search until I find the right screwdriver for a towel bar. I grab some light bulbs and a ladder for Charlie's office. Grandpa keeps his keys on a hidden hook that only the two of us know about. I grab them and walk upstairs. With the jingling key ring, I feel like a pro.

I go to Charlie's office first so I can ditch the ladder. Unlike Grandpa's office, Charlie's is super-organized. There's not a paper out of place. File folders are stacked neatly in bins and his pens all have caps and are facing in the same direction in a ceramic pen pot that one of his kids must have made.

The light bulbs are an easy fix and I'm folding the ladder up when I notice something on Charlie's desk that makes me pause. It's lying right in plain sight, so I'm not snooping or anything. It's a printed-out e-mail and it's the first line that catches my eye: *Position: Head Custodian of Brayside Retirement Villa.*

That's Grandpa's job.

I pick up the paper and read the whole thing. It's a job posting. The hair on my arms prickles. Is Charlie looking to replace Grandpa?

Warning bells go off in my head. All the meetings Grandpa's had lately, were they about keeping his job? I put the paper back down exactly where I found it, turn off the lights, and close the door. But I know that for the rest of the evening it's all I'll be thinking about.

Chapter 29

Maggie

Through the glass doors, Maggie can see Artie at the front desk and Austin dusting. She'd left school as soon as the dismissal bell rang, not bothering to go to her locker in case Brianne and Lexi were waiting for her.

"What are you doing here?" Austin blurts when Maggie steps inside. "I mean, it's Monday."

Maggie shrugs. A blush creeps up her neck. "I wanted to know what happened with the puppy," she admits. "And to help Mrs. Fradette. Or work in the library. If that's okay?" She looks past Austin to Artie.

"No argument from me," he says. "Hey, guess what Mrs. Fradette did earlier this afternoon?" He chuckles as he tells them. "Hijacked the bridge club and taught them Texas Hold'em!"

Maggie grins thinking about sweet Mrs. O'Brien scooping up poker chips from Mrs. Kowalski and Miss Lin.

"Who won?" Austin asks.

"Mrs. Kowalski. She made out like a bandit. Mrs. O'Brien is baking her muffins for a month!"

The phone at the front desk rings and Artie answers it, leaving Austin and Maggie alone.

"Any news about the puppy?" Maggie asks.

"The lady at the shelter said she was lucky Harvey found her when he did."

Maggie leaves Austin to his dusting and heads to Mrs. Fradette's suite. She knocks on the door. "It's Maggie— Margaret," she corrects herself.

"Come in," Mrs. Fradette calls out. "It's open."

Mrs. Fradette is standing at the kitchen counter. "What good timing you have. I was just about to make some tea." Without asking, she pulls a cup out for Maggie. "I hope you like orange pekoe. My daughter-in-law sends it from England."

Mrs. Fradette brings the cup of tea to Maggie and sets it down on the kitchen table, which is covered with photos. "Still working on your collage?" Maggie asks.

"I haven't gone through these photos in years," Mrs.

Fradette says, picking one up. "Remember I told you about my grandparents in Laurier? This is them."

Maggie looks closer at the small black-and-white photo of two unsmiling old people. They are sitting on the veranda of a clapboard house.

"My grandma, Mémère we called her, struck the fear of God into all of us. She refused to speak English and had a wooden spoon hanging on a hook in the kitchen. We all knew what it was for. That spring in Laurier she used it a fair bit on Michel!" Mrs. Fradette grins. "Mémère thought Mom was too easy on us, I think. But Pépère was kind, very soft-spoken." She sifts through the photos and finds one to show Maggie. "That's him."

Her grandpa was tall with a long face and dark hair. Mrs. Fradette looks at the photo for another moment and adds it to a small pile. "And here's one of him with his car. It was a dark green 1942 Plymouth." The car in the photo has a domed roof and curved wheel wells. It reminds Maggie of a larger version of a VW Beetle. "Ronny and I used to climb in and pretend to drive it. I think we flooded the engine a few times, but Pépère never got mad at us."

"He didn't use the wooden spoon?" Maggie asks, half joking.

Mrs. Fradette cackles. "Oh no! Not Pépère. He never even raised his voice. He was a mechanic. His shop was across the field from the house. It's because of him my life took the turn that it did. Well, him and the flood, I suppose."

"What do you mean?" Maggie asks. She takes a sip of her tea. It is bitter and strong, but Maggie kind of likes it.

Mrs. Fradette finds the photo of the garage again. "You see, this side"—she points to the side with the closed door—"was filled with old cars. There was a pickup truck with a Model T front and flat back. Oh, and there was another brown car I remember, from the 1930s. And a powder-blue Ford. Now that was a beauty. Everything smelled like diesel fuel and rust and I loved it."

Mrs. Fradette's face glows as she talks about it. "I'd scramble around exploring, imagining what it would be like to bring the cars to life again. When I was younger and we visited in summer, he'd let me help him in the garage now and then. He called me his assistant.

"Over breakfast on our first morning of the evacuation, I asked Pépère if I could go with him to the garage. The last thing I wanted was to be stuck at home with Mémère and Mom. I'd be given chores, or worse, told to look after my little brother and sister.

"Pépère grinned and took a long sip of his coffee. ''Course you can,' he said. Mom raised her eyebrows at him, but didn't say anything. She knew I was looking for any excuse to get out of the house.

"When we got to the garage, Pépère set me up on a stool. I watched while he laid out his tools. My cousin Alphonse arrived for work at nine o'clock. Alphonse was sixteen and the oldest of Aunt Cecile and Uncle Joe's boys. School was done for him and he'd chosen to work at the garage with Pépère. I'd never had much to do with Alphonse before. I remember he didn't look too happy to see me hanging around. 'What's she doing here?' he asked.

"'She's learning,' Pépère answered.

"'She's not going to learn much, just sitting there,' Alphonse muttered. He probably hoped I'd get bored and scamper away, but that garage had always fascinated me and now that we were in Laurier for a while, I wasn't going to let him scare me off. Besides, I adored Pépère. When I was little, Mom called me his shadow because I was always following him around.

"Pépère stood up and scratched his head. 'That's a good point.' Pépère walked over to me and put a wrench in my hand.

"I stared at it. I'd never even held a tool. It was heavy. 'That's a crescent wrench,' he said. 'Come here and I'll show you how to use it.' Poor Alphonse turned away muttering, curse words probably, but too low for Pépère to hear them. My clothes were covered in grease by the time lunch rolled around.

"Mom's eyes turned to saucers when Pépère and I walked into the kitchen for lunch. 'Josephine! What have you done?' she said." Mrs. Fradette breaks off with a laugh. She slaps her knee and cackles. "Oh! My poor mother! But Pépère didn't miss a beat. 'She's helping in the garage.' As if it was the most natural thing in the world. Pépère was a kind man, but he had a steel will too. There was no budging him when his mind was made up. Mom didn't even argue. She just shook her head. 'Go wash up, then.' But under her breath she muttered, 'Wait till your father hears about this.'"

"Did your dad find out?" Maggie asks.

"Oh, of course! He called every day to give us an update on the house. We still hadn't flooded, but things hadn't gotten any better. Ronny was staying over at Uncle Wilfred and Aunt Winnie's, so Mom called them every other day to check in on him. He and some of the other Scouts had been taught to drive motorboats. They'd patrol the banks of the dikes looking for breaks, or help with evacuations if needed.

"The men were getting tired after weeks and weeks of working almost twenty-four hours a day. Dad had taken to sleeping on the couch in the living room with one arm dangling off the edge. He figured he'd wake up if he could feel the water.

"I guess I should have thanked the flood for preoccupying Dad. He was so busy trying to save our house that when he found out later that night that his daughter was working at a garage it didn't bother him half as much as it should have."

There's another photo of Mrs. Fradette, standing beside an old truck. Her dark hair is pulled back in a ponytail and she's wearing overalls. She's got her hands on her hips, head tilted like she's asking the photographer a question. "I was so free up there," she says. "It wasn't like at home." She looks at the photo wistfully. "I could just be me."

Maggie is filled with a sudden longing. She can't quite put her finger on it, but she'd like to know what "just being me" feels like.

When it's time for Maggie to leave, she finds Austin is at the entrance. He's moved on from dusting to washing the windows. No wonder he likes it when Harvey comes to visit. He does more chores in a week at Brayside than Maggie's ever done at home. "How's Mrs. Fradette?" he asks.

"Still working on her collage," Maggie says. "It's taking her forever, but I think she likes looking at all the photos."

"Old people aren't big on rushing. Except Mr. Singh, but that's just because he has his Cobra GT4."

Maggie smiles. "She still has things in boxes, but every time I go to help her, she starts telling me stories." Maggie glances at the front window. Her dad had texted that he would be there in a few minutes.

"Mr. Pickering was like that too."

Outside the dining room, Maggie notices a wreath of flowers, the kind you order for a funeral. "Is that for Mr. Stephens?" she asks.

Austin shakes his head. "No. He's out of the hospital. It's for a different lady. Someone from the third floor. I didn't know her."

Before Maggie came to Brayside, she imagined it as a place where death hung in the air like a bad smell. But it isn't like that at all, at least not on the first floor. All the old people are so lively. Especially Mrs. Fradette. "I thought being around old people would make me sad." Maggie gives the wreath a meaningful look. "But it doesn't. At least it hasn't so far."

Austin nods. "I couldn't come to Brayside for a while after Mr. Pickering died. But when I did, everyone here understood. They all missed him too. He was ready though, when he died. And it was because of Harvey."

Maggie frowns, confused.

"Meeting Harvey reminded him of his dog, General. That's why he started talking to me. I know I should have done more to find you. It was wrong to keep Harvey, but giving him back meant—"

"The end of talking with Mr. Pickering."

For a year, Maggie has let her anger over Harvey's disappearance fester. But she sees now, she had it wrong. Austin wasn't trying to hurt her when he kept Harvey, he was trying to help an old man.

When her dad pulls up outside, Maggie is once again reluctant to leave. There's something she needs to say to Austin. "I'm glad it was you who found Harvey," she says.

Any remnants of guilt that had been hovering between them disappear. "Are you coming back tomorrow?" Austin asks.

Maggie thinks for a minute. Why not? "I'm going to try," she says, and waves goodbye.

Chapter 30
Austin

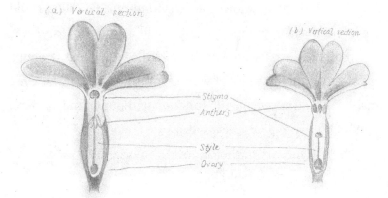

(a) Vertical section

(b) Vertical section

Stigma

Anthers

Style

Ovary

"Is Grandpa happy at Brayside?" I ask my mom over dinner. "I think so. Why?"

I focus on my food, worried I'll give away what I'm really worried about. *Is Grandpa going to lose his job?* "How old is he now, anyway?"

"He'll be sixty-three in December."

He's old, but not that old. "Do you think he'll want to retire soon?"

Mom shakes her head. "I can't imagine Grandpa retired. What would he do with himself?" Hearing Mom's words does nothing to make me feel better.

After dinner, I'm supposed to be labeling the parts of a plant for science, but I can't concentrate. Finding that job posting on Charlie's desk has me all twisted up. On the one hand, I think I should tell Grandpa, warn him that his job is on the line.

But on the other hand, if I tell Grandpa what I found, Charlie will want to know how he found out. Grandpa could get in trouble for snooping. Or be mad at me because *I* was snooping. It doesn't seem fair that Charlie would toss Grandpa out after seventeen years of working at Brayside. I can't even imagine how Brayside would function without Grandpa there.

Which is what gives me an idea.

I have to make Charlie see how important Grandpa is to Brayside. But I can't do it alone.

Chapter 31

Harvey

There is always a walk before Maggie calls Harvey upstairs and he curls up on her bed for her bedtime. This evening is no different. Maggie pulls Harvey away from the sliding doors, where he has kept watch for the last hour. She clips the leash to his harness and they go out the front door. They usually walk to the end of the street and back.

As soon as he is outside, Harvey takes deep sniffs of the sidewalk and grass. He detects nothing out of the ordinary. All the scents he picks up catalog neatly into his brain. Rosie, the Westie who lives a few doors down, has been out recently. The fire hydrant is sprinkled with her odor. He adds some of his own scent and in this way communicates that he has been here too.

Harvey walks with his ears pricked, rotating to capture sounds like an old-fashioned satellite dish. "Yoda ears," Maggie's dad calls them. They are useful in times like this, when danger might be nearby. Harvey hears car tires rotating on pavement and the hum of car engines. Dry leaves crunch under Maggie's soft-soled shoes behind him. All noises Harvey expects on an evening walk. And then, there is a crash. Harvey freezes. Every hair stands on end. He gives a low, warning growl.

"It's just a garbage can lid," Maggie says.

Harvey won't move. He listens intently. *What is out there?* "Come on, Harvey." Maggie moves in front of him and yanks on the leash to get him moving. Unlike Harvey, she is not bothered by the noise, or by what might be out there. Harvey follows, but stays alert.

Before he goes inside the house, he pauses and surveils the front yard. It is his duty to protect his territory and his Maggie. If there is an intruder Harvey won't rest until he sniffs it out and sends it away.

Or dies trying.

Chapter 32

Maggie

Mrs. Weston holds the sign-up sheet in her hands. She looks around at the girls at their desks, with their disinterested faces. Another class and another group of blank stares.

"So, no one wants to enter this contest?" Hope leaks out of Mrs. Weston's voice and Maggie cringes for her.

The sign-up sheet is for a historical essay contest. Mrs. Weston has explained that every year, the call goes out for submissions and that there is a prize. Not only does the winner receive a

$100 gift card to a bookstore, but their paper is published in the Historical Society's magazine.

"And, of course, you'll have bragging rights," Mrs. Weston says grinning.

Maggie is doing her best to keep her eyes on her desk. As soon as Mrs. Weston mentioned the contest, an idea popped into her head. It might be crazy to even pursue it, so she keeps quiet. At least, until lunch hour.

Maggie is sitting with Lexi and Brianne at their usual table in the cafeteria. It has been a week since the Student Leadership Committee meeting and there is an uneasy truce between them. Maggie picks her words carefully, and does more sitting and listening than usual. Lexi was elected as seventh-grade rep, so Maggie's failure to vote has been forgiven.

Lexi and Brianne are discussing a new series released on Netflix which they both binge-watched on the weekend. Maggie hasn't seen it yet and zones out. "What did you do on the weekend?" Brianne asks Maggie. "If you weren't watching Netflix."

"More volunteer hours?" Lexi asks. The barbed comment is not lost on Maggie.

"I did other stuff too," Maggie says a little defensively. But then struggles with what that other stuff was. Brianne and Lexi wait expectantly. "I took Harvey for a walk," she says quietly, realizing how pathetic it sounds.

"Oh, Mags!" Brianne says, shaking her head. Maggie grits her teeth at her friend's condescending tone.

"I know you think Brayside sounds boring, but it really isn't." She'd like to add that she thinks staying inside all weekend to watch TV sounds boring too, but she doesn't.

The girls wrinkle their noses and Maggie feels like she's been left out of a conversation. Her last shift at Brayside was spent in the library, which now looks more like a library. Maggie was asked to play piano before lunch again and Austin taught Harvey a new trick. All in all, it was an enjoyable afternoon.

Lexi ducks her head like she's trying to hide. "Oh no! Mrs. Weston is here."

"Why is that bad?" Maggie whispers. She thought they liked Mrs. Weston.

"She's super-intense about this essay contest. She caught me in the hallway and wants me to 'think seriously about entering.'"

"As if we have time!" Brianne moans. "We get so much homework!"

"You had time to watch a whole series on Netflix," Maggie points out, but regrets the comment when she gets *the stare* from her friends.

"That's different. That's downtime. And when did you become my mom?"

"You're turning into an old person! From spending so much time at Brayside!" Brianne snickers.

Maggie smiles at the comment and tries not to take it personally. She's just teasing, she reminds herself. But it also makes her wary about admitting she has an essay idea, or that she's considering entering. It will give them another reason to mock her.

Despite Lexi's attempt to hide, Mrs. Weston sees them and walks over. She still has the sign-up sheet in her hand and it is still blank. "Hi girls!" she says. "I know I talked about the contest in class, but I wanted to double-check that none of you wanted to enter. The deadline is pretty soon, so if you're interested…" She lets her voice trail off.

"Sorry." Brianne shakes her head.

Mrs. Weston turns to Lexi. "Lexi?" she says hopefully. "I know you said no earlier…"

"It's not really my thing," Lexi says with a shrug.

Mrs. Weston turns to Maggie.

Maggie's idea has been percolating all morning. But with her friends watching her, she can't admit that she'd like to enter. So, instead, she shakes her head regretfully. "All right, well, if you change your mind"—Mrs. Weston holds up the sheet—"you know where to find me."

The girls watch as Mrs. Weston moves on to the next table of seventh graders. "I wouldn't even know what to write about, anyway," Brianne says. "History's pretty boring. It all happened so long ago. Like, who cares?"

The answer to Brianne's question burns on Maggie's

tongue. History is not boring and there are plenty of reasons to care. But their friendship is already on shaky ground. She doesn't want to look like a keener, so she bites back her words and tries to look interested as the conversation returns to Netflix.

Chapter 33

Austin

I bump into Charlie. I'm arriving as he's leaving. The thing about Charlie is he's really cheap. He's happy to have me around as long as he doesn't have to pay me. He's also a perfectionist and wants everything at Brayside to look top-notch all the time, which is why it's such a classy place. "The planters out front need to be watered," he says to me. "And the laundry room door is squeaking. Maybe you could oil it."

Charlie is short and has thinning brown hair. He wears a suit every day and moves like he's always in a rush. Personally, I think he should stop and talk to the old people more often. But Grandpa says he's an administrator, not a caregiver and there's a big difference. "Charlie has to drive the bus. It's Mary Rose's job to look after the passengers."

"What's your job?" I asked, grinning.

"I keep the engine running," he said, and winked at me. Lately, Charlie's always rushing off to meetings, so I'm surprised when he stops in the hallway and looks me in the eye. "Your grandpa was telling me what an independent worker you are. He says the residents are just as happy to see you with a tool kit as him. It's nice to see a young person eager to learn."

Charlie hardly ever talks to me. It makes me worried he's buttering me up before he fires Grandpa. "Grandpa's just being nice. He's the one with all the skill."

"No doubt there," Charlie says. "You'll always be welcome here, Austin, whether your grandpa's here or not."

I stare at him as he waves goodbye to me and to Louise, who's at reception. A sick feeling churns in my gut. It's the same feeling I had earlier today when I looked at the science test I barely studied for. "Did you hear what he said?" I ask Louise.

"Charlie?" she asks, flipping through pages on a clipboard. "I don't listen to half of what he says."

"He's going to fire him."

"Fire who?" She puts the clipboard down and gives me her full attention. "Austin, are you okay?"

"He's going to fire Grandpa."

Louise's eyes double in size. "He's gonna what?"

"I found the job posting on his desk," I say miserably. I wish I'd never found it. Knowing and not being able to tell Grandpa is like not being able to spit a bad taste out of my mouth.

"Why would he fire Phillip?"

"Because he's old. He could probably hire someone younger for half the money."

Louise pulls up a stool to the reception and plunks down on it. I rest my head in my hands. "Did you say anything to Phillip?" she asks me.

"No."

"Good. You leave this with me. I'll get to the bottom of it. No one's getting rid of your grandpa without my say-so. You got that?" She fixes me with one of her no-nonsense looks, the kind that the residents know not to mess with.

All I can do is give a weak nod.

"Austin!" Mr. Santos bursts out of his room waving a newspaper.

"He's been waiting for you all afternoon," Louise whispers. "Won't even tell me the clue. Said you're the only one he asks for help."

"Apple with buds. Four letters. Ends with a *D*. I think."

I don't have to think very long before I say, "iPod?" He stands at the desk and writes in the letters.

"I could have got that one," Louise mutters to me under her breath. "Crossword genius, my heinie."

Chapter 34

"What a nice surprise," Mrs. O'Brien says when Maggie shows up after school. "But no Harvey today?" With her white hair and rosy cheeks, Mrs. O'Brien looks like one of the ladies who dress up as Mrs. Claus at the mall, minus the tacky red dress.

Maggie shakes her head. "He's at home. I'll bring him on the weekend though."

"He was funny the other day. Full of beans! Come by my room on your way out. I have some muffins with your name on them." Maggie promises she will, and heads over to Mrs. Fradette's suite.

Last night, Maggie gave more thought to the essay contest. The topic is Hidden History. She is sure that Mrs. Fradette's stories about leaving Winnipeg during the flood would make a great essay topic. She just has to figure out an angle. What made Mrs. Fradette's experiences unusual?

She knows it's a long shot, but she can't help thinking how exciting it would be to win. Wouldn't Mrs. Fradette love to see her story in print? Mrs. Fradette answers the door as if she'd been waiting on the other side of it.

"Margaret! Come and see what I finally finished." Mrs. Fradette opens the door to her suite wider so Maggie can join her. The mess of photos on the kitchen table is gone and Mrs. Fradette has completed not one but three frames of photos from her life. "The problem was trying to choose photos for just one frame," she explained. "So I said to heck with it and made three."

Maggie grins at her. "Good thinking."

The photos are arranged chronologically, Maggie notices. The ones at the top of the first frame are from when Mrs. Fradette was young. The photo of her family at the train station is there. Halfway down Mrs. Fradette has included a photo of her in a pale dress standing beside a man in a suit. "Is that your wedding day?" Maggie asks.

"Yes. That was Bert. He's been gone a long time now," Mrs. Fradette says wistfully. Maggie scans to the bottom and there is a recent photo of Mrs. Fradette sitting in a chair at what must have been her old home, surrounded by her son and his children. But in between are a multitude of memories.

Maggie sits down in the kitchen chair and Mrs. Fradette pulls up a chair beside her. Maggie feels a bit like an archaeologist, but instead of digging for artifacts (and with the essay contest on her mind), she is searching for stories. Mrs. Fradette grins eagerly as her eyes run over the pictures she's spent the last few days agonizing over. "That's Pépère and Henri, his tomcat."

Maggie looks at the black cat. Part of one ear is missing. "I don't know who adopted who, but Henri came home with Pépère one day and that was it. He wasn't like most cats: he never left Pépère's side. He even slept under Pépère's bed. Mémère tolerated him because he caught mice in the house."

Maggie smiles, thinking that Henri sounds more like a dog than a cat.

"Henri went to the garage every day with Pépère. There was an old chair out front of the garage that Henri slept on. When a customer pulled up, he'd meow loudly. Pépère used to call him his doorbell."

Mrs. Fradette tilts her head, looking at the photo. "He didn't let anyone but Pépère and me pat him," she says proudly. "He'd hiss at everyone else."

"Why?" Maggie asks.

Mrs. Fradette leans back in her chair and Maggie can tell she's in for a story. "The Lacroix family, who lived near my grandparents, had a son about my age. Norm was his name." Mrs. Fradette says the name with disdain. "He'd pass the garage on his way home from school and toss stones at Henri. Henri would hiss, or howl if Norm actually hit him, but by the time Pépère got out there, Norm would either have run off, or would have his hands in his pockets, whistling as he walked by like he'd done nothing wrong. It used to drive Pépère crazy!

"One day, I was out front and saw Norm coming before he saw me. I picked up some rocks from the ground and crouched behind the corner, waiting. He took a look around and pulled a stone from his pocket. He didn't have a chance to let it fly though." Even though it was seventy years ago, Mrs. Fradette still has a look of glee on her face. "I let one of my rocks fly and nailed him right in the gut!"

"Oh no!" Maggie laughs. She can imagine the mischievous dark-haired girl from the photos chucking the rock and smirking when it hit its mark.

"Norm clutched his stomach. 'I've been shot!' he cried, and fell to the ground. Pépère and Alphonse came racing out of the garage.

"'What happened?' Pépère said, looking around.

"'Am I bleeding? Is it bad? Am I gonna die?' Norm was screaming, more with the shock of it than from actually being hurt." Mrs. Fradette isn't just telling the story anymore, she's animated, using different voices for each of the people, including a light French accent for Pépère.

"'Alphonse, take him home, will you?' Pépère said.

"Alphonse rolled his eyes at Norm's theatrics. He wasn't too happy about helping Norm home, but he hauled the boy up and let him lean on his shoulder. The Lacroix family was well-off and their first son was older than Alphonse. He made a big show of driving his new car up and down the main street. I'd caught my cousin staring at him enviously more than once.

"As Norm limped away with Alphonse, I figured I was in the clear until Pépère rounded on me. 'Do you know what happened to that boy?'

"I still had a rock in my hand and let it drop to the ground at my feet. 'You can't throw rocks at people,' Pépère said, bending over so we were eye to eye. 'Even when they deserve it. Mean can't be solved with more mean. Okay?' I hung my head. I didn't like disappointing him.

"Pépère didn't mention anything about it to Mom, which was a good thing. She might not have let me go with him to the garage anymore if she knew I was throwing rocks at boys. Although she was so worried about the flood, I'm not sure she would have paid much attention. The radio was always on and as soon as the news broadcast started, Mom turned it up to listen. She and my dad agreed to a daily six o'clock phone call. If the call didn't come, she'd fly into a panic and call Uncle Wilfred's house, assuming the worst.

"It might have been the same day I threw the rock at Norm Lacroix that we heard on the radio that the dike along Wellington Crescent had broken."

Maggie has been listening intently and raises her eyebrows. "When Dad called that night he told us that there was water right up to the front doors of St. Ambrose. I did my best to hide my excitement, but thought my prayers had been answered. Maybe the school would be shut down permanently! No more nuns! No more disapproving looks! Of course, my prayers weren't answered. The school only suffered minimal damage. We saw a photograph in the newspaper a few days later of two nuns paddling in a canoe past the school gates! In their habits!" She laughs at the memory.

"What about your house?"

"It was still safe. The Lyndale dike was holding, but the water was lapping at the top. All it would take was another inch or two and we'd be done for. All of this sailed over my head, to be honest. I was so caught up in working at the garage. Without the constraints of school, the layers peeled off me. I was a grease rat." And then she cackles, slapping her hand on her thigh. "Truly, I was. With each passing day, I was becoming more and more at home in that garage."

Mrs. Fradette is interrupted by a knock on the door. One of the nurse's aides is there. "Blood pressure check," she says brightly. Maggie catches the flash of irritation on Mrs. Fradette's face.

"I guess I should get going," Maggie says reluctantly. She still has a lot of work to get done in the library and less and less time to do it.

"I'll see you tomorrow," Mrs. Fradette says, as if her return is a given.

Chapter 35
Harvey

Maggie's fingers are tapping on the keyboard when Harvey goes to her and stretches so his front paws are on her leg. "Not now, Harvs," Maggie says. "I'm researching." Harvey, of course, doesn't know what "researching" is, but she does rub her hand over his head and scratch under his collar in a most pleasing way before she turns back to her computer. "Or trying to," she mumbles.

Harvey sits for a few minutes at her feet, hoping for some attention. When none comes, Harvey wanders downstairs, where he paws at the sliding door until Maggie's mom lets him out.

As soon as Harvey steps into the backyard, his black nose quivers. Just as Maggie might take in all the colors of a painting at once with her eyes, Harvey's nose is attuned to every scent the air holds. Harvey raises his head. There is one that stands out.

Curious, Harvey cases the perimeter, trying to locate its source. He weaves in and out of plants in the garden and circles trees. He sprinkles his scent in key locations. With his curiosity piqued, Harvey is reluctant to head indoors. But as it grows late, the promise of warmth inside and food in his bowl lures him back to the sliding door. A breeze blows over Harvey's white coat, ruffling his fur. It carries the scent of leaf mold and fallen apples, of goose feathers and pinecones.

And something else.

Downwind the creature is stirring, emerging from under a rotten log.

Like Harvey, she has instincts too, and they are telling her that her current home will not do for the coming winter. She's on the hunt for something better. More comfortable and better protected.

Perhaps a hollowed-out space where she can curl up and sleep for a few weeks when it gets cold. A gap beneath a shed will do nicely.

She's not worried about the threat of another animal. She flexes her sharp claws and arches her humped back. The fur bristles. She too has a small black nose finely tuned to decipher scents. She catches Harvey's odor. He's well-groomed, so his scent carries none of her untamed, forest smells.

The raccoon isn't looking for a fight, but she's a survivor. She doesn't have an owner to care for her or protect her, or a warmly lit home to retreat to. She will be patient and stalk the space until the right moment arises for her to make a move.

But one thing is for sure. No curious little dog is going to get in her way.

Chapter 36
Austin

My palms were sweating by the time I got to Brayside. I'd come up with a plan to save Grandpa's job. It wasn't that complicated; it was the going-behind-his-back part that kept me up at night. In the end, it wasn't me who was going to save his job anyway, it was a bunch of old people.

I'd run through the what-ifs. What if they didn't want to? I mean, some of them had been retired for over twenty years or had never worked at all. What if they thought not working would be good for Grandpa?

What if they didn't want any part of this plan? They lived

at Brayside because it made their lives easier and here I was complicating it.

But the scariest what-if was: What if Charlie was right? What if Grandpa wasn't doing a good job? Maybe his age was catching up with him and I hadn't noticed?

"Hey, Austin," Artie says. He's got Mrs. Kowalski in a wheelchair.

I do a double take because that's not usual for her. "What happened?"

"Took a bit of a tumble this morning," Artie says. "Her ankle is sprained."

"Bob left his slippers right in the middle of the floor," she grumbles. "I could've broken a hip!" It's true. Old people's bones are brittle. Grandpa says when old people fall they don't bounce like I do; they often break bones. A broken hip is bad news for them. I've seen a few people go straight up to the second floor after that injury.

"But don't worry, Austin. Artie's bringing me into the games room early so I can get a seat at the front." It's hard to keep a secret at Brayside. I told Louise my plan yesterday, which means by now everyone will have heard it. Seeing Mrs. Kowalski so committed lifts my spirits. All the what-ifs fade away.

"Louise and I went door-to-door this morning," Artie says. "To let everyone know. We posted a sign too." He nods to the activities bulletin board where a black-and-white computer-printed sign is taped up. FREE BAKE GOODS is in big letters and underneath it reads: *Join us in the Games Room for a resident sing-along!*

"The free baking was Mrs. O'Brien's idea. She's been making muffins all day."

Mrs. Kowalski turns in the chair to look at me. "Listen, dear. We're going to do everything we can to make sure things stay the same around here." She gives me an encouraging smile.

"Where's Charlie?" I ask.

"Louise took a peek at his schedule. He left for a meeting earlier today and won't be back."

"And Grandpa?"

"Don't worry about him. He hates sing-alongs. He'll hide in his office till it's over."

The sliding glass doors open and a guy in khaki pants and a button-up shirt walks through. He's got a paper in his hand and a nervous look about him. He smooths his hair down and pulls at his sleeves.

"Can I help you?" Artie asks.

"Is the manager here?"

"Sorry, he's not. Something I can help you with?"

"I saw the posting for the custodian job," the guy says with a nervous smile. "Thought I'd come by and introduce myself. I'm Isaac." He holds out his hand to Artie, who takes it. Warning bells are going off in my head. This young guy is Grandpa's competition. About thirty years old, fit and tidy. Is he the kind of person Charlie wants working at Brayside?

The three of us stare at him until it gets uncomfortable. "The position is filled," Mrs. Kowalski says.

Isaac's face falls. "But the posting said it was open until—" "It's filled," she says, looking as authoritative as a woman wearing a housecoat and slippers can.

Isaac puts the paper down on the desk anyway. "I'll leave this in case another job becomes available. You can keep it on file." He's talking to Mrs. Kowalski like she's in charge. Then he turns and leaves.

As soon as the sliding doors whoosh shut behind him, Louise comes out of the staff room and frowns at the three of us. "What did I miss?"

"That guy was applying for Phillip's job," Artie says.

"He's the third one today." She pulls a file folder out of the top drawer of the reception desk. She's about to add Isaac's résumé to them, but instead she does something that I never would have expected Louise to do. She puts the résumés straight into the paper shredder.

"Louise!" I say.

"Your grandpa would do the same for me, Austin. We look out for our own around here." I want to hug her and when I look at Artie and Mrs. Kowalski, they're both nodding in agreement.

Old people like to be early for things, so it doesn't take long for the games room to fill up. Artie puts Mrs. Kowalski's wheelchair right at the front and leaves a chair beside it for her husband. Mrs. O'Brien comes in next with a plate of muffins. Miss Lin and Mrs. Luzzi are behind her and each of them has a plate of cookies.

I wrote out a couple of things on loose-leaf so I wouldn't forget anything. My hands tremble as I take it out of my pocket. It's silly that I'm so nervous since I see these people almost every day, but there's so much on the line right now. If my plan doesn't work, I don't know what Grandpa will do. Who is going to hire a guy his age? He needs his job and not just because of the money. He likes to work because that's who he is.

The residents look at me kindly, smiling and nodding. By the time Louise has herded them all into seats, lining up wheelchairs and walkers, the room is crowded. Mr. Singh scooters himself right up to the front and gives me a big thumbs-up.

Mr. Santos works on a crossword while we're waiting to start. At the back, Louise nods for me to begin. I clear my throat and open my mouth.

But there's a creak as the door opens, so I stop. What if it's Grandpa?

Everyone turns as Mrs. Fradette and Maggie slip in.

Mrs. Gelman purses her lips at the late arrival, but points to the empty chair beside her, which Mrs. Fradette takes. Maggie stays standing at the back beside Artie and Louise.

Maggie gives me a big smile and for some reason seeing her there makes me braver. I clear my throat again and start talking.

"Hi, everyone." Instead of silence like at school when I have to give a presentation, all the old people say hello back to me. This also makes my nerves disappear. "So, I guess you figured out there's no sing-along." There's a murmur of laughter. "What I wanted to talk to you about is my grandpa. I found out that his job is posted and Charlie's been accepting résumés." Lots of white-haired heads shake. "What I was hoping is that if everyone wrote a letter to Charlie explaining how important Grandpa is to Brayside he'd change his mind."

"Of course we will, dear!" Mrs. Luzzi says.

"I've already started one," Mr. Singh adds.

"What if he wants to go?" Everyone turns to look at Mrs. Fradette. "Have you asked him?"

"Well, no."

"Phillip's still a young man," Mr. Santos, who's in his eighties, says.

"He's never said anything about retiring to me or my mom," I explain. "He still likes coming to work. He never complains, even if he has to come in on the weekends." It's true. Brayside has a weekend custodian to do the cleaning, but if there is a plumbing or electrical issue, Charlie knows he can call on Grandpa because he'll come to fix it.

Louise pipes up from the back. "I've known Phillip since he started here. If he wanted to retire, we'd have talked about it."

"When do you want the letters written?" Mrs. O'Brien asks. "As soon as possible, I guess. Is tomorrow okay?"

From the back of the room, Maggie speaks up. "If you need help, I can type them on the computer in the library."

I give her a big smile of gratitude.

For the first time since I found the job posting on Charlie's desk, I breathe easier. Grandpa might not be a spring chicken, but he's not on the chopping block either.

Chapter 37

Maggie

M aggie's mind drifts off as her math teacher hands back a test. "What'd you get?" Brianne asks, turning around in her desk. Her thumb is placed strategically over her mark.

"Eighty-five percent," Maggie says. It's a good mark, but based on the satisfied smirk on her friend's face, she can tell it's not as good as Brianne's. Usually, this would bother her. She'd hide her test, quickly slipping it into her binder, or go through every question and grade-grub for a few more points to boost her final mark.

But this time, when Brianne shows her the 90% circled on her paper, Maggie gives her a half-hearted congratulatory smile. Then she goes back to thinking about Mrs. Fradette, the essay contest, and Brayside.

She typed up four letters yesterday after Austin's speech. She'd thought the old people would write about how well Phillip did his job.

But that wasn't what happened at all.

Each letter was a tribute, a little story about some way Phillip had helped each of them. Some were funny and others touching. As Maggie typed them up, she realized the residents at Brayside were as much a family as she, her sisters, and her parents.

When Maggie had got home last night, she'd filled in her chart of volunteer hours. All the time she'd spent at Brayside after school and on the weekends had already added up to seventeen hours. Only three more hours? Maggie frowned. She wasn't ready to be done with Brayside.

With all the talk about Phillip's job, there hadn't been much time for her to visit with Mrs. Fradette, but she'd been giving the essay some thought. Something Mrs. Fradette had said the other day about being a "grease monkey" had intrigued her. A girl working in a garage in the 1950s must have been unusual. Even now it was rare to see a female mechanic. Could that be the nugget she's looking for?

At lunch the next day, Maggie lets out a sigh of relief when she sees that her seat next to Lexi and Brianne is still vacant. She's a few minutes late because she was talking to Mrs. Weston about the essay contest.

"Where were you?" Lexi asks.

"Talking with Mrs. Weston," Maggie says, sitting down.

"About?" Brianne asks.

The truth sits deep in Maggie's throat. It isn't just the itchy socks and the uniform that are different now that she's in seventh grade. Qualities that used to be commended in elementary school, like wanting to enter an essay contest, have suddenly become embarrassing. "My mom thinks I need help with English." Maggie gives a convincing eye roll.

Both girls groan in sympathy. Maggie silently congratulates herself. The lie has given her an excuse to see Mrs. Weston without Brianne and Lexi asking questions. When she'd spoken with Mrs. Weston today, she'd told her about Mrs. Fradette and the things she was learning about the flood evacuation. "I want to use her stories for the essay contest," Maggie had said to Mrs. Weston.

"The topic is Hidden History so find one unusual area to focus on," Mrs. Weston had replied. "Something people won't know much about. And think about what her story is teaching you."

As Brianne and Lexi discuss another seventh grader's unfortunate haircut, Maggie drifts off again, preoccupied with thoughts of her essay and Mrs. Fradette.

Chapter 38

Austin

All my worries about the old people not wanting to write letters flew from my mind when I got to Brayside the next day. "Hello" is barely out of my mouth before Louise grabs my hand and leads me around to the back of the nurse's station to show me the stack of letters she is hiding in a drawer. A bunch of them are typed, thanks to Maggie, and others are handwritten. One, from Mr. Santos, is three pages long.

I'm not sure what to say, but finally sputter, "Wow!"

"I know!" Louise says. "One of them says, 'It will be the biggest regret of your professional career if you let Phillip go.'" She hoots with laughter.

"You've been reading them?"

Louise gives me a sly look. "Of course. And this didn't come a moment too soon. Look at what came today." She passes me a résumé and I skim it.

"'Jerry Zubick. Head custodian for Park View Manor,'" I read out loud. Park View is a place a lot like Brayside. I keep reading and see that he's got twenty years of experience and is also a licensed electrician. This applicant isn't a newbie like Isaac. Jerry could be real competition for Grandpa.

"I can't keep shredding the applications either. Charlie's getting suspicious. He keeps asking if there's any more mail than what's on his desk. I think we need another sing-along," Louise says. "But this time, Charlie needs to be there. Just passing the letters on isn't enough. He needs to hear from the residents. If he saw how much Phillip means to them—" Louise waves her hand and shakes her head.

"Okay," I say slowly, "but how are we going to get Charlie there?"

Louise doesn't have a chance to answer because I hear Grandpa's key ring jangling. I stuff Jerry's résumé and the letters back into the drawer. "Hey, Grandpa. Everything okay?" I ask as he comes to the front desk.

When he frowns, his forehead gets even more wrinkles. "Yeah. I was just talking with Charlie," he says, looking at Louise more than me.

"About what?" I get all tingly with nerves. What if Charlie fires Grandpa before I can give him the letters?

He opens his mouth, then closes it and shakes his head. "Nothing for you to worry about. Come on. You've got some work to do in Mrs. Gelman's suite. I'm going to show you how to re-caulk a tub."

I shoot Louise a look. She gives it right back. Between the two of us, we've got to come up with something, and quick! On the way to Mrs. Gelman's suite, I glance at the Kowalskis' photo collage. The center picture is the two of them under a FIFTIETH ANNIVERSARY banner.

And that's when I get my idea.

I slap my forehead like I've forgotten something. "Shoot! I was supposed to help Mr. Santos with today's puzzle. I'll meet you in Mrs. Gelman's in a few minutes."

Grandpa nods and I wait around the corner until he's inside her suite. Louise looks up from her charts when I slap my hands on the front desk. "We'll tell Charlie it's a surprise party for Grandpa. For his seventeenth anniversary at Brayside."

"How do you know when he started?

"I don't. Not exactly anyway. The point is that Charlie will have to come to the party. When all the old people are there, we'll have them read their letters. There's no way Charlie will let him go after all that. He'd look like the world's biggest jerk."

A grin spreads across Louise's face. "I'll make up the invitations tonight. We'll have the party tomorrow before dinner in the games room. I'll ask the chef to make a cake."

I head back to Mrs. Gelman's suite. Grandpa hasn't even started on the shower yet. He's been chatting with Mrs. Gelman. She's grinning so big, I'm worried her dentures are going to fall out. "I'll make you some latkes tomorrow," she says. Grandpa is so much more than just a custodian to Brayside. How can Charlie not see that?

Well, after tomorrow, Charlie will see. I just hope that it's not too late.

Chapter 39

Maggie

Maggie hadn't planned on coming to Brayside today, but she found something last night when she was researching that she couldn't wait to share with Mrs. Fradette.

When she gets to Mrs. Fradette's door, it's already open. Inside, Louise is sitting on the couch with a blood pressure gauge around Mrs. Fradette's arm. Not wanting to intrude, Maggie goes back to the hallway and waits.

The three collages have been hung and they take up most of the wall space between Mrs. Fradette's suite and Miss Lin's. There are so many photos that every time Maggie looks, she notices a new one.

Today, her eyes are drawn to a particularly blurry photo. It looks like Mrs. Fradette is standing beside a baby deer. Maggie looks closer. Spindly legs, long neck; the head is the right shape. Maggie wonders what the story is behind that photo.

Maggie peeks into Mrs. Fradette's suite to see if Louise is finished. "It's high," Louise says, pulling the stethoscope out of her ears. "You have to take it easy."

Mrs. Fradette waves a hand at Louise. "I'm eighty-three. I haven't taken it easy my whole life, I'm not starting now."

Maggie is relieved to hear Mrs. Fradette still feisty. She can't be feeling that bad. Maggie raps lightly on the door to announce her arrival. "Mrs. Fradette?" she calls. "It's Margaret."

It is Louise who gestures for her to come in. "Perfect! Maggie can keep you company. I'll be back in an hour." Louise turns to Mrs. Fradette with a stern look. "And you need to keep resting. Maggie can get you whatever you need."

As soon as Louise is gone, Mrs. Fradette sits up. "Getting old is no fun, Margaret. No matter how well you tune the engine, something's always breaking down."

"It's important to have a good mechanic," Maggie says with a grin.

Mrs. Fradette gives one of her barky laughs. "Exactly!" Mrs. Fradette plumps the pillow behind her. The apartment is looking more organized. A few ornaments have been unpacked and stored in a cabinet. Framed photos of grandkids sit beside a lamp on the end table, and books have been placed on a shelf.

Maggie wonders if unpacking is what raised Mrs. Fradette's blood pressure.

"My son called today," Mrs. Fradette says. "He wanted a photo of my car so he could write up an ad. He says there's a website that sells cars like mine."

"Did you send him one?"

"I'm still thinking about it," Mrs. Fradette says. "I just can't imagine someone else driving her."

Maggie watches Mrs. Fradette carefully. Maybe it is thinking about selling her car that raises her blood pressure, not the unpacking. "There's no rush to decide, is there?"

Mrs. Fradette considers Maggie's words. "No, I guess there isn't. I have a parking spot and insurance is taken care of." Her face relaxes.

Maggie reaches into her backpack. "I found something for you. On the internet." Maggie hands Mrs. Fradette a printed-out photograph of the nuns canoeing on the St. Ambrose school grounds. She'd searched for it on a whim, knowing Mrs. Fradette would get a kick out of it.

"Oh goodness! Oh my!" Mrs. Fradette laughs. "There they are!" She looks at the photo as if it is a long-lost friend.

Maggie sits down on the couch beside her. She can smell Mrs. Fradette's perfume and sees the slight tremble in her hands.

"Seeing this takes me right back to Mémère's kitchen. Every day when the paper came, Mom would spread it out on the table. All the articles were about the flood. Things in

Winnipeg were tense. Dad had taken to calling himself a 'flood bachelor,' which Mom didn't like at all. Dad said some of the neighborhoods he patrolled were ghost towns as the water kept creeping up. The Lyndale dike had held, but the whole city was holding its breath, waiting for the water to go one way or the other.

"There were new concerns to worry about now too. Kids getting sick because of dirty drinking water. Some children were being sent away even if their parents had to stay."

Maggie frowns as she listens.

"More and more, my mom was relieved we'd left when we did, but she worried about Ronny. She wanted Dad to send him up by train, but he wouldn't leave. I didn't blame him. It must have been exciting ferrying people out of their flooded houses in the motorboats. All those Scouts were being put to good use. But for me, Laurier was where I wanted to be."

She smiles at Maggie, but it's a tired smile and Maggie worries she's wearing her out with the talking. "Do you want anything?" Maggie asks. "Some water? A rest?"

Mrs. Fradette shakes her head. "No, I'm fine. It's just so nice to have company. All the other ladies are jealous you come to visit me." Mrs. Fradette winks at Maggie. "It's why I haven't been in a rush to unpack. If it's all done, you won't have a reason to visit!"

Mrs. Fradette says it in a teasing way, but Maggie is filled with a rush of tenderness for the old lady. "I'd still visit,"

Maggie says. "There was a photo in the collage. It looked like you were standing with a baby deer." Maggie half expects Mrs. Fradette to frown at her, confused.

Instead, she says, "Oh yes, that was my fawn, Peggy."

"You had a pet deer?" For anyone else, this question would be absurd, but not for Mrs. Fradette.

Mrs. Fradette nods. "She thought she was a pet anyway. She went everywhere with me."

"How did—?" Maggie doesn't quite get the whole sentence out before Mrs. Fradette fluffs the pillow behind her back and starts talking again. Maggie settles in to listen.

Chapter 40

Maggie

"Pépère and I were driving on a gravel road. It had stormed the day before and the road was full of potholes. Pépère had to drive along the shoulder to stay clear of them. That was when I spotted something in the ditch. At first, I thought it was a dog and asked Pépère to pull over. I jumped out of the truck and made my way down into the ditch to where she was, this little brown thing, curled up into a ball.

"I bent down to get a better look. Her eyes were open wide and she was shivering. 'It's not a dog,' I shouted to Pépère. 'It's a fawn!' Pépère came to have a look. She wasn't a newborn, but she was very young, still had her white spots. I crouched down and let her sniff my hand. 'Something must have happened to the mother,' I said.

"She didn't try to run, maybe because she was too weak or too scared, so I reached out and touched the bridge of her nose. She didn't flinch. Her hair was velvety soft but her nose was dry as a bone and I said so to Pépère. She was going to die if we didn't feed her.

"I could tell Pépère didn't like the idea of interrupting the natural course of things. 'We can't take her with us,' he said gently.

"'Why not?'

"Pépère ran a hand over his chin. He did that a lot when he was thinking about something. 'She's a wild animal, Josephine.'

"'So's Henri,' I pointed out. 'At least he was until you took him in.'

"'He's a cat. This is a deer.'

"'She's going to die if we leave her here,' I said again. I stroked her head and she looked up at me, grateful. With her legs curled under her she didn't look any bigger than Henri. 'I'm not going without her,' I said." Mrs. Fradette shakes her head. "I meant it too. Poor Pépère. He didn't stand a chance.

"Pépère sighed. 'All right. Can you pick her up?'

"I nodded and put one hand under her neck and the other behind her legs. She didn't weigh much—she was all legs. I could feel her heart fluttering a mile a minute. Pépère opened the gate to the truck and helped me up. I sat down and held the deer in my lap. Weak and scared, she didn't stir once.

"'I'll go slow,' Pépère said. 'Hold on.'" Mrs. Fradette sits back, a faint smile on her lips. Maggie doesn't say anything, letting her enjoy the memory.

"When we got home, Pépère went inside and explained to my mom and Mémère what had happened. Mom came out of the house shaking her head at me. But Mémère brought a bowl of milk and lay it on the veranda. I carried the deer up the front steps and sat down with her. She settled against me like she was my own child.

"I pulled the bowl of milk closer. Mémère knelt down and showed me how to dip my finger in the milk and hold it to the fawn's mouth to give her a taste for it. It wasn't long before she was sucking the milk off my finger.

"'Josephine,' my mom warned. 'It's not staying. Don't get attached.'

'She'll be less work than Michel,' I said. 'Anyway, there's no fence back here. She's free to go when she's strong enough.' Oh, I was a sassy thing, wasn't I?" Mrs. Fradette looks at Maggie, who smiles and nods in confirmation.

"I named her Peggy. Leggy Peggy was what Pépère called her. I didn't go into the garage that day. I was content to sit out on the veranda nursing her back to health. She made little mewling noises while she slept and tucked her nose under a leg, curled up as tight as can be. I already felt like I was her mama."

Maggie thinks back to Harvey's puppy days, when he was still so new and she was responsible for keeping him safe and fed and warm.

"I didn't want to leave her alone when night came, but Mom insisted I sleep inside. I packed a quilt around her for warmth, even though I was sure she'd be gone in the morning. But when I woke up, there she was! Sleeping on the veranda, just where I'd left her."

"She didn't want to leave," Maggie says, smiling.

Mrs. Fradette nods. "After a few days, she was strong enough to drink on her own. Pépère figured she was about two weeks old by the way she was starting to forage. She'd follow me to the garage sometimes and chase moths in the field. That was how Norm Lacroix found out about her."

Maggie's mouth tightens at the mention of Norm Lacroix, the boy who threw the rock at Henri. She waits for more, but Mrs. Fradette lies back on her pillow and lets out a long breath, as if she's just run a marathon. "I'm a little worn out today."

"I've kept you talking too long," Maggie says guiltily.

"It's not your fault. I've just got an old motor. Besides, I like telling these stories. It's good to remember the good and the bad." Mrs. Fradette sits up and swings first one leg, then the other to the ground. It's an action that Maggie could do in one smooth motion, but for Mrs. Fradette, it requires effort. "I think I'll go lie down."

Maggie stands up too and takes Mrs. Fradette's arm, even though she hasn't asked for help. Together they walk into the bedroom. On the bedside table is a glass of water and a wedding photo in a silver frame. Maggie lowers Mrs. Fradette to the bed and covers her legs with a quilt.

"You're a kind girl, Margaret. Thank you." Her eyes are closed before Maggie leaves the room.

In the hallway, Maggie looks again at the photo of Mrs. Fradette and Peggy. Something about the way Mrs. Fradette is telling the story makes Maggie think it's not going to end well for Peggy. She made a comment about remembering good and bad memories; and that horrible Norm Lacroix is back too.

With a final glance at the photo, Maggie heads to the library, thoughts of Laurier, a twelve-year old Josephine, and Peggy dancing in her head.

When Maggie gets home from Brayside, she heads to her room with Harvey at her heels. He curls up on her bed while she sits at her desk and turns on her computer. She's researching garages in the 1950s. Only a few minutes later, she gets a text.

Who wants to go to Tubby's tmw? Lexi's text reads. Tubby's is a pizza place and the hangout for St. Ambrose students.

Bri replies *Yes* right away, but Maggie stares at the text, hesitating. She knows she should be relieved to be included.

She's part of the trio again. But if she goes she'll miss the surprise party for Austin's grandpa at Brayside. After typing up the letters and seeing how much he means to the residents, she doesn't want to miss it.

And trying to explain that to her friends, who already think she's weird for enjoying her time at Brayside, feels impossible.

So, instead of responding, she turns her phone over and ignores the text. It's cowardly, and she knows it. A voice that sounds an awful lot like Mrs. Fradette's tells her if they are really her friends, they'll understand, but another voice reminds her that she's already on shaky ground. Another misstep and she'll tumble off the ledge. Maggie sighs. It's a no-win situation. She glances at Harvey. He's curled up on her bed with her sock in his mouth. He worked hard to yank it off her foot and now won't let it go. She wishes her life could be as worry-free as his.

Her phone beeps with a text. *Are you coming or not?* It's from Lexi but in a group chat with Brianne.

IDK, Maggie replies.

Why not?

I might have other plans.

Maggie hesitates before pressing the send button. It's a lame reply, vague. Would Lexi press her for details? Or leave it alone?

Lexi: *OMG. Not the old people!*

Brianne: *LOL. Would you like us more if we had walkers?*

Lexi: *White hair?*

Brianne: *Adult diapers?*

Lexi and Brianne think it's a joke. They have no idea what it's like hearing Mrs. Fradette's stories. If they did, they wouldn't make fun of her. Maggie tosses her phone on her bed, narrowly missing Harvey. He sits up, startled.

Is she being too sensitive, or are they being hurtful on purpose?

They'd invited her to join them, but she doesn't feel part of them the way she used to. Maggie realizes the truth of what's bothering her, and it has nothing to do with their comments. Maybe she's outgrowing them, and not the other way around.

Chapter 41

Harvey

Despite looking comfortable on Maggie's bed, Harvey is unsettled. All around him, things are different.

First, there is the matter of outside. Despite his best efforts to pee in every corner, and keeping a vigilant watch at the sliding doors, something is still coming into his yard. He could smell it when he was let out in the morning.

Then there is the change in his Maggie. She used to carry herself lightly. Her steps skipped and Harvey had to be quick to keep up. Now, her feet are heavy. Her gait is weighted down, thoughtful.

An air of burden swims around his Maggie and Harvey doesn't know how to make it go away. Today, when she came home, Harvey ran to the door to greet her, jumping with excitement at her return. Harvey has no sense of time. Her absence could have been five minutes or five hours and his reaction would have been the same. Harvey wants nothing more than to be with his Maggie.

Maggie says a quick hello to her mom and goes upstairs to her room with Harvey at her heels. Harvey would love a walk and gently nips at her fingers while she's patting him. "Not now, Harvs," Maggie says. "I have stuff to do."

She sits down at her desk, then pulls notebooks and pens out of her backpack. Harvey isn't ready to give up. He sniffs out Maggie's feet and starts to yank on one sock, determined to pull it off. The wiggling toes surprise and delight him, but what he really wants is that tasty sock. Maggie giggles and kicks her feet away. Spurred on by her laughter, he redoubles his efforts, digging his hind legs in and clamping his teeth on the stretchy fabric. A sock will be his!

After working hard, he's rewarded and leaps up onto Maggie's bed with one sock dangling out of his mouth. He lies down so he can keep an eye on her. From under his feathery white lashes he sees her check her phone and make a noise of disappointment, the same sound he gets when he has an accident on the carpet. He lifts his head. Has he done something wrong? Maggie keeps staring at her phone. Even from where he sits on the bed, he can feel her body tense. His Maggie is angry. She tosses her phone to the bed, narrowly missing Harvey.

Chapter 42

Maggie

When Maggie sees the girls at their lockers on Thursday morning, she behaves as she normally does, and is met with silence. They talk to each other as if she isn't there. And while they don't mention last night's text-versation, Maggie knows it is why they are ignoring her. Imagining the things that were said behind her back gives her a stomachache. Three has never been a good number—too many sharp corners, and now Maggie is the odd one out.

She grits her teeth all morning, but by lunch can't take it anymore. She considers calling her mom to ask if she can go home, but then she won't be allowed to go to Brayside. So she seeks refuge in the school library, sneaking bites of her sandwich at the computer station. At locker breaks, she times her steps carefully and manages to continue evading the girls.

On a whim, she checks the website for the shelter where Austin took the puppy. There are lots of adoptable dogs, mostly large ones. The puppy isn't listed. Is it because it's still too young, or, and Maggie hates to think this, did it not survive? The puppy had the odds stacked against it. Maybe that was why Harvey was so protective? He knew it didn't have long to live?

At the end of the day, Maggie grabs her backpack and leaves, anxious to get to Brayside. At least there, she always feels welcome.

Chapter 43

Austin

Concentrating at school isn't easy for me most days, but this afternoon it was impossible. With the fake work-iversary party looming, all I could think about was what would happen if Grandpa found out.

And then the what-ifs started to sneak back in. *What if it doesn't work? What if I'm too late?*

Getting fired from Brayside would be the ultimate betrayal for Grandpa. He's given so much to that place. It's more than just a job; the residents are like family to him. By the time I get to Brayside after school, I'm a nervous wreck.

"Where is he?" I whisper to Louise. She gives me a

conspiratorial wink as I stash my backpack behind the reception desk.

"I sent your grandpa to Mr. Santos' room. He's going to keep him busy while we get set up." I wince at the thought of being stuck with Mr. Santos until five o'clock. Grandpa might actually want to take forced retirement after the sixty minutes are up.

"And I told him he has to come to the sing-along today. He mumbled something about being tone deaf, but I told him Mrs. O'Brien had baked something special for him."

"Good thinking," I say.

A familiar SUV pulls up to the curb outside and a minute later a ball of scruffy white fur races inside, followed by Maggie. "I asked my mom if she'd let me bring him today," Maggie explains, unclipping his leash from his collar. "Your grandpa was really nice to him when he was lost. I thought he should be here."

Harvey's tail is wagging so fast his butt levitates off the ground. I laugh and bury my hands in the fur between his ears, then down his back. When I look at Maggie, I expect to see her smiling too, but she's not. "Everything okay?" I ask. Something is wrong. Even her hair doesn't look as bright as usual.

Maggie gives a one-shoulder shrug. "School sucked today." I know how that feels. "Did you do bad on a test?" I ask.

She shakes her head. "My friends are mad at me." Maggie bites her lips, hesitating. "They wanted me to hang out with them at Tubby's Pizza Place, but instead I came here."

"But you couldn't go! It's the party."

"Exactly!" She looks relieved that I see her side of it. "I can go to Tubby's anytime."

Maggie doesn't have to explain to me what she gets out of being at Brayside. "Maybe you could bring them sometime? They could meet Mrs. Fradette."

Maggie snorts. "I can't even imagine suggesting that to Lexi."

What kind of friends do you have? I wonder, and when I look at her face, I know she's thinking the same thing.

"I'll be in Mrs. Fradette's room," she says. "Let me know if you need help with anything. I'll bring Harvey with me so he isn't in the way."

Harvey follows Maggie down the hall. Mary Rose shows up carrying a tray of cups. She nods to the dining room. "I just checked in with Mr. Santos. He's showing Phillip his stamp collection. Your poor grandpa." She shakes her head, laughing.

"At least now the sing-along won't seem so bad," I point out.

Mrs. O'Brien appears with a tray of cookies, including the double-chocolate ones Grandpa likes the best. Miss Lin has made paper flowers for all the tables that match the tablecloths and napkins. On the back wall, Louise hung up a banner that says: HAPPY ANNIVERSARY. Lots of residents mill around chatting with one another. There's never been a surprise party at Brayside that I know of and they're buzzing about it.

"I didn't want to be late. It takes me a good five minutes to get down that hallway with my walker," I hear Mrs. Luzzi say when she comes in.

"Not me. Fifteen seconds, door to door," boasts Mr. Singh. The party doesn't start for another forty-five minutes, but they're all here, waiting for Grandpa. Waiting to tell him how much they want him to stay.

Chapter 44

Maggie

Maggie wouldn't tell her mom what was wrong when her mom picked her up from school. She's not sure why she told Austin, but she's glad she did. Would her mom have understood the way he had? She doesn't think so. She has no regrets about choosing Brayside over Tubby's, but she is worried about what the future will hold for her friendship with Lexi and Brianne.

These thoughts weigh heavily on her as she and Harvey arrive at Mrs. Fradette's door. When Mrs. Fradette answers, Harvey stands tall, as if he's ready for inspection. "You look nice," Maggie gushes. Mrs. Fradette is wearing her signature red lipstick and a red dress to match.

"I got all tiddled up for the party!" Mrs. Fradette says. "You've brought your dog." She holds out her fingers for Harvey to sniff. He tucks his tail between his legs and inches closer.

"You're feeling better?" Maggie says, although she can tell that she is.

"Just needed a little rest. The move to Brayside has been more tiring than I expected."

She gestures for Maggie to sit down, so she takes a seat on the couch. Harvey lies right at her feet, his head on his paws. "He's very loyal to you, isn't he?" Mrs. Fradette asks, nodding at Harvey.

"I'm his person," Maggie says with a shrug. Harvey gives a contented sigh.

"Peggy was like that. Acted more like a dog than a deer. Whenever she saw me, she'd run over and nuzzle me, like a colt would. If I sat down, she'd curl up right beside me and sometimes put her head in my lap. It was the sweetest thing." Mrs. Fradette's face softens at the memory.

"'She's wild, you know,' Pépère reminded me one morning. He was drinking his coffee on the verandah. The rockers of his chair creaked against the wooden floor. 'Not a pet.'

"'So's Henri.' I shot back. 'And you keep him.' I was like that, with an answer for everything.

"Pépère smirked. 'He stays with me because he wants to, not because he has to. This fawn—'

"'Peggy,' I interrupted.

"'This fawn,' he said again, 'needs to survive on her own. You can't keep her. What's going to happen when you go back to Winnipeg?'

"I didn't have an answer. Pépère's reminder that I'd have to go back to Winnipeg one day was like a bucket of ice water. It put me in a foul mood and I wouldn't answer him. I was still surly when we walked to the garage later on, which didn't help the situation with Norm Lacroix.

"Ever since I threw that rock at him, he and a gang of boys would walk past the garage on the way home from school. They stood on the other side of the road so someone walking by wouldn't have thought anything of it, but I knew they were trying to intimidate me. They'd lean against the fence and watch me work."

Even as she tells the story now, years after it happened, Mrs. Fradette's body tenses with fiery energy. "I decided it was time to fight fire with fire. There were all kinds of tools in the garage. Chemicals too. And the hoist for lifting cars. It was a dangerous place. They wanted to intimidate me?" Mrs. Fradette snorts with laughter. "I'd show them intimidation! I pulled out Pépère's welding torch. It was connected to the tanks with a long hose. I'd seen him use it a few times and watched while he'd trained Alphonse on it. It didn't look any different than the kerosene lamps we used for camping. I turned the knob that opened the acetylene and oxygen tanks.

You should have seen the boys scatter when I came at them with a lit welding torch! I couldn't go very far since I was attached to the tanks, but they didn't know that! They took off down the road like a bunch of scared rabbits!" Maggie giggles along with Mrs. Fradette at the memory.

"Well, guess who comes sneaking back a little while later? Norm Lacroix! He came behind the garage, through the field. There were car parts and a few rusted-out cars out there in the tall grass. Peggy loved it; perfect for grazing. Henri liked it in the field because he could stalk field mice.

"Norm might have been trying to scare me, but when Henri raced into the garage, I knew something detestable was out there. My first thought was a dog, but then I remembered a lone fawn was an invitation for a coyote. I dropped what I was doing and ran out back. Norm was staring at Peggy. When she saw me, she walked over on her spindly legs and stood at my side.

"'You got a deer?' he said. Curiosity was plain on his face.

"'What's it to you?' I asked. 'And why are you here, anyway?'

"'I came to tell you to stay away from my friends.'

"I hooted with laughter. With his red face and balled-up fists, he was the last person I was going to take orders from. 'It's you and your friends who need to stay away from me.'

"He stuck out his chin and glared at me with his tiny, piggish eyes. I got a chill when he turned to Peggy and fixed her with the same look.

"'What're doing with that deer anyway?'

"'None of your business,' I said. But Norm wouldn't let it go. "'She just wandered into your yard, or what?'

"'I found her,' I said. Peggy hadn't left my side while we were talking. She positioned half her body behind me and peeked out at Norm. 'Anything else you want to know?' I put my hands on my hips and scowled at him." Mrs. Fradette demonstrates, giving Maggie the same nasty look. "He stomped back through the grass to the main road. Henri gave a yowl of good riddance, but Peggy stared after him as if she knew he couldn't be trusted.

"I thought that was the end of it until Norm's father pulled into the garage just as Pépère was closing up for the day. He stepped out of the car and slammed the door shut. 'That girl's a danger,' he said, pointing at me. Norm had gotten his small close-set eyes from his father. They were sunk deep into his face and had the same nasty glint in them.

"'How do you mean?' Pépère asked. Of course he knew about the rock, but he hadn't seen me with the welding torch.

"'She tried to set my son on fire today.'

"Pépère knew what kind of a boy Norm was and he was probably thinking the boy deserved it. But he also knew what kind of a girl I was." Mrs. Fradette winks at Maggie. "'What was your boy doing hanging around the garage anyway?' Pépère asked. 'He's got no business here.'

"Lacroix laughed. Honest to goodness, he sounded like a

villain from the radio programs we used to listen to. 'The rest of the town would sure hate to hear that your garage was employing a girl who's been unkind to my son.'

"Being the only garage in town was a blessing and a curse. Pépère got all Laurier's business, but crossing the wrong person could spell disaster. Mr. Lacroix was a businessman and had influence. If he started bad-mouthing Pépère, people might take their business to Ste. Rose.

"'You keep your boy away from my garage and we won't have any trouble,' Pépère said. Then his tone changed. He pulled a rag out of his coveralls pocket and wiped his hands with it. 'Why don't you bring your car by tomorrow. I'll do an oil change for free.'

"Lacroix looked at Pépère like it might be a trick. Pépère raised his eyebrows, waiting for Lacroix to answer.

"Lacroix glanced at me. 'Don't let her near the car,' he said.

"Pépère nodded and turned and went back into the garage. I waited until Lacroix had driven off before I spoke. 'Why'd you offer to do the oil change? His son is the problem, not me. I was just defending myself.'

"'A man like him needs to leave feeling like he's won. An oil change isn't going to take more than half an hour. A bad relation ship with him will last a lifetime.'"

Mrs. Fradette pauses, but only for a moment. "It was good advice. I think Pépère taught me as much about dealing with people as about fixing cars. But it was the cars I was crazy for.

Engines made sense to me in a way reading and writing and arithmetic never did. I liked getting my hands dirty. Pépère let me tinker with the broken-down cars in the shed attached to the garage. I'd go to bed thinking about them, planning how I'd get them running again.

"This was all fine and dandy while we were in Laurier, but I was worried about what would happen when the flood was over and we went back to Winnipeg. How could I return to being a St. Ambrose student when I knew in my heart that I was meant to be covered in grit and grease in a garage? It kept me up at night, that's how much I dreaded going home. All my worries came to a head one night."

Chapter 45

Maggie

When Mrs. Fradette pauses, Maggie is at the edge of her seat. *Don't stop*, she silently pleads. Harvey stirs at her feet, but only to reposition himself. Mrs. Fradette smiles at him, takes a breath and continues.

"Like I told you before, Dad called every evening at six o'clock. Mom busied herself in the kitchen waiting for the phone to ring. The radio had said things were improving in Winnipeg, but we'd heard that before. No one believed the reports anyway. They weren't fortune-tellers. That river had a mind of its own and all we could do was stand back, watching and waiting.

"Only this one night, the call never came.

"The first thing Mom did was call Uncle Wilfred's house. If anyone knew where Dad and Ronny were, it would be he and Aunt Winnie. She called their place, but there was no answer there either. Mom flew into a tizzy. She wouldn't let herself cry, not in front of us, but she kept wringing her hands and praying under her breath. There'd only been one death in Winnipeg due to the flood, but if the Lyndale dike had blown, well, who knew what might have happened.

"Part of me wanted to escape outside. There was nothing I could do to help Mom anyway. I was about to sneak out to see Peggy when there was a knock on the door.

"I'd seen the wartime movies when a soldier comes to a house to report a fallen comrade. And honestly, that was my first thought. The flood was the enemy and my dad was its victim. He'd sacrificed himself to save our home.

"Mémère looked at Mom across the kitchen where she stood frozen. I wished Pépère were there, but he was still at the garage, or so I thought. If the worst had happened, well, we'd need him with us.

"The knock came again. I couldn't stand the suspense, so I went to the door and swung it open. 'I thought no one was home!' Dad's voice boomed with laughter.

"Mom flew across the room and clobbered him with a hug. Everyone started laughing and asking questions. Then Ronny showed his face too and behind them both was Pépère."

Mrs. Fradette pauses and smiles at the memory. Maggie finds that she is also grinning. She bends down and pats Harvey on the head. "They surprised you."

"They sure did. Dad and Pépère had worked it all out. As of the night before, the river level had gone down. The dike had held and our house was safe. My poor dad though. 'Haggard' doesn't begin to describe his appearance. The fact that the first thing he wanted to do was be reunited with his family taught me something about him that day that I'd never have guessed at before. Mom couldn't get close enough to him and for one of the first times in my life, I saw them share a kiss. Not just a peck on the cheek, either. A movie star kiss that left Mom gasping and weak in the knees. It made me blush to see my parents do that." Mrs. Fradette gives one of her trademark cackles at the memory.

"Even though Dad and Ronny were exhausted, Aunt Cecile and Uncle Joe came over with their brood to celebrate. We were loud, all of us. Uncle Joe brought his fiddle, which hadn't come out since I'd been there, and it turned into a proper kitchen party with dancing and drinking. It was good to see Ronny too. He'd become a different person since I'd been in Laurier, but I think he would have said the same about me.

"Later on, the two of us were sitting on the floor with our backs against the wall since all the grown-ups had the chairs. 'Looking forward to coming home?' Ronny asked.

"'Not really,' I confessed.

"'You want to stay here with Mémère?' Ronny used to joke that her sour face could curdle cream.

"'She's not that bad,' I told him. Since we'd been living with them, I'd seen a different side of her. She looked after Peggy, making sure her water bowl was full, and never complained about the extra work we'd made for her. 'I just don't see the point in going back.' I knew by then that I didn't want to be a nurse or a teacher, or any of the things other little girls thought about. There was no other job I wanted to do as much as work with cars. 'I want to stay here and work with Pépère. I want to be a mechanic.'"

Maggie had known this epiphany was coming. But to hear Mrs. Fradette say it out loud makes Maggie want to cheer for her. This part of the story is exactly what she's been waiting for. She can feel an essay blooming in her mind: "The Hidden History of a 1950s Female Mechanic."

"I see your smile, Margaret. Just because I wanted something didn't mean it was going to happen. It was still 1950 and I was girl. There were no female mechanics. It wasn't even a possibility for me."

"What did you do?" Maggie knows Mrs. Fradette can't have given up. But she doesn't find out, because Mrs. Fradette looks at the clock. "The party starts soon. Maybe we should save the rest of this story for another day."

It pains Maggie to think of leaving the story there. Did Mrs. Fradette actually abandon her dreams?

Mrs. Fradette stands up. "Shall we?" As she and Maggie go to the door, Mrs. Fradette looks at Harvey, who has roused himself from the floor with a yawn and a stretch. "He's a sweet dog," she says.

Maggie looks down at Harvey. It's hard not to smile at him. He looks so pleased with himself as he holds his tail high and trots ahead of them down the hallway. Maggie thinks she is lucky to have Harvey, and to have met Mrs. Fradette.

Chapter 46

Austin

If you ask an old person how they're doing, you have to be prepared to listen to the answer. I made that mistake with Mrs. Gelman and heard about her sciatica for five minutes. It could have been worse. Mr. Kowalski has hemorrhoids.

"I think everyone's here," Louise says. We've got enough chairs and Artie is guarding the food. Charlie just called. He's on his way."

"Where was he?" I ask.

"At some building site a few blocks away. Said he'd be here in ten minutes."

My palms are sweaty waiting for Grandpa. Mrs. Fradette and

Maggie come in with Harvey. He makes the rounds, greeting everyone who calls him over. He especially loves Mrs. O'Brien, but that's probably because she slips him baking when no one's looking. Maggie doesn't look as bummed out as she did when she got here, so maybe the visit with Mrs. Fradette cheered her up.

Louise passes me the stack of letters from all the old people. "After we yell 'surprise,' you can call people up to read their letters."

Things are going according to plan until I hear Mr. Santos shouting in the hallway. "Wait! Phillip! We were only on Zambia! I still have all of Zimbabwe to show you."

"Oh no! Places everyone!" I whisper-yell. No one moves. They can't hear me above the chatter. I catch Maggie's eye across the room. "He's coming!" I say more loudly.

But half the people can't hear well, and the other half can't move well, so watching everyone try to find a chair is like watching a slow-motion game of musical chairs. The plan was for Louise to turn off the lights, but I can see now there's no way a dark room with a bunch of old people is a good idea. Finally, Louise takes control. "Stay where you are!" she shouts. "He's coming!"

When the door to the games room opens, it's not exactly how I pictured it. We didn't practice the yelling-surprise part, so no one does. Instead, we stare at Grandpa, who looks more uncomfortable than surprised.

"Sorry, Austin. I did my best," Mr. Santos puffs from behind him. His straggly comb-over is flopping onto the wrong side of his head.

Mary Rose shouts, "Three, two, one—" And then everyone yells, "Surprise!" sort of at the same time.

Grandpa looks confused. "Is it my birthday?" he asks.

"It's your work-iversary. You've been working here for seventeen years," Mary Rose tells him. She brings over a golden crown and places it on his head.

"Have I?" he says with a chuckle. "Feels like just yesterday." That gets a laugh from the other old people.

"We wanted to throw you a party. Make sure you knew how much we appreciate what you do around here," Louise says.

Grandpa waves the compliment away. "Just doing my job." Mr. Santos nudges Grandpa inside and behind them Charlie appears. "Sorry I'm late," he says. "Did I miss the surprise part?"

Louise purses her lips and crosses her arms over her chest. "Mm-hmm," she says, unimpressed.

"You knew about this?" Grandpa asks Charlie.

"I found out about it yesterday," he says.

"Come on, Grandpa. Now that Charlie's here, we can get started." I grab Grandpa's hand and pull him to a chair at the front. Mary Rose put some streamers on it so the guests would know it was reserved. "Hi, everyone," I say from the front. I sort of yell-speak because Mr. Kowalski won't be able to hear me otherwise. "To celebrate my grandpa's years of working at Brayside, everyone here wanted to tell him how important he is to this place." I look right at Charlie when I say these words. "First is Miss Lin."

Miss Lin is so tiny that when she gets to the front, instead of asking if everyone can hear her, she says, "Can everyone see me?" and laughs.

"Some of you will remember my sister, Patty. She and I spoke every day at three o'clock. When she passed away, I didn't have my three o'clock phone call to look forward to. But Phillip started coming by. Some days, I didn't even talk, but he stayed, just sitting with me. And some days I needed to cry and he let me do that too. I found out later from one of the nurses that he waited until three o'clock to take his lunch break so he could spend it with me." Miss Lin pauses. She's got tears in her eyes. "That's what I have to tell you, Phillip. Thank you for not letting me feel alone. You were there when I needed you the most." Miss Lin goes back to her seat and on the way gives Grandpa a hug.

A few more people get up to talk and then it's Mrs. Kowalski. She straightens her stretchy floral shirt and clears her throat. "I'd like to tell you about the day we moved in. Bob didn't want to come here. He hated giving up the house, but it was time." There are a few understanding nods from the crowd. "Phillip came by and he could tell right away that Bob wasn't happy. Soon as he found out that Bob was a carpenter, he let him set up a shop in the basement here. Well, Bob had all his tools over here lickety-split. Phillip had him building bookshelves and shoe racks. It kept him busy and out of my hair. Thank you for getting to know us, Phillip. You're a special man."

I peek at Grandpa. He's looking around like he can't believe all this is for him.

Then Mrs. O'Brien gets up to read her letter. "Most of you know this story already, but it bears repeating. Here goes." She takes a big breath. "Five years ago, I had a heart attack. It was Phillip who found me. He said he just had a feeling as he was walking by my room. When he knocked and I didn't answer right away, he called for a nurse. The doctors said if it had been a few more minutes, I'd be gone.

"I don't know what kind of an angel you are, Phillip, but you saved my life. I think you save everyone's life at Brayside in one way or another, in little ways. Knowing when we need a smile or a visit. You're a skilled custodian, but it's your compassion that makes you a perfect fit for Brayside."

Louise had warned me that some of the letters were touching, but I wasn't prepared for Mrs. O'Brien words. She didn't even read from a sheet of paper —all her words came straight from her heart. She looks right at Grandpa and says, "Phillip, you know how much you mean to me. If it hadn't been for you, I might not be here."

Grandpa waves a hand at her, like it's all no big deal, but his chin is trembling and then he puts his hand to his mouth.

"And you know what they say," Mrs. O'Brien continues. "The proof is in the pudding. Look who organized this whole thing—your grandson! All the kindness you've shown to others is coming back to you. Brayside wouldn't be the same without you, Phillip."

Everyone claps and that gives me a minute to pull myself together. A bunch of other people are dabbing their eyes too. "Thanks, Mrs. O'Brien," I say. I look at Charlie across the room. He's got a puzzled look on his face. I bet he's regretting his decision to post Grandpa's job.

Finally, when all the letters have been read, Grandpa stands up. He blows his nose into his hankie and stuffs it in the pocket of his coveralls. "I can't believe you all did this," he says. "I never expected—well, I guess I didn't realize how much a part of this place I really am." He looks at me and blinks back tears. "That's why saying what I have to say is so difficult."

There's a hush in the room like everyone's holding their breath at the exact same moment.

"Charlie and I, well, we decided it was time—"

"You can't fire him!" I shout. All the emotion bottled up in me from listening to how much the residents love Grandpa comes gushing out at once. "You can't! Didn't you hear what everyone said?" I glare at Charlie.

"Austin!" Grandpa says my name so sharply, I turn, startled. "No one's firing me! I got a promotion!"

A promotion?

Grandpa shakes his head at me. "The owners of Brayside

are building a new complex. Like Brayside, only bigger. They need a head custodian with experience. I've taken the job."

There's a long, awkward pause. A few of the residents clap for Grandpa and others want to know where the new building is, but everyone is smiling. They're happy for him.

I'm still standing at the front trying to make sense of what he said. "A promotion?"

He nods.

"So the job posting…?"

"Was for me to hire my replacement. The pickings have been slim, to tell you the truth. I'm going to have to work at both places unless we get a good candidate. Or any candidate."

Louise and I look at each other across the room. Her eyes go wide and my cheeks turn red. "Uh, Grandpa." While I explain, Louise puts on some music and Artie cuts the cake. Grandpa shakes his head at what happened when Isaac tried to apply, then starts chuckling, and finally is belly-laughing. The kind that you can't not laugh with.

"You did that all for me?" he says when he can breathe. "And then put together this party?"

I shrug, still embarrassed. His face gets all thoughtful and he pulls me against him. He opens his mouth to say something, but no words come out. I can feel the tremor in his chest and I know that it's not laughing that's doing that.

"I'd do anything for you, Grandpa," I whisper. And even if my voice was too quiet, he heard me. Loud and clear.

Chapter 47

Harvey

Harvey enjoys parties. He likes the activity and the smells, but mostly, he likes the crumbs that are dropped on the floor. He spends most of the time under the food table. Maggie's mother calls him Hoover for good reason.

As people drift away from the games room, Harvey follows Maggie when she goes to talk to Austin. "Do you need any more help cleaning up?" she asks. The recycling and garbage bins are piled with paper plates and cups.

Austin shakes his head and bends down to give Harvey some attention. "Things didn't turn out how I thought they would," he says with a laugh. "I got the surprise, not Grandpa!"

"I can't believe he's really leaving," Maggie says.

"Yeah, me neither."

When the head scratch is over, Harvey wanders away. There are so many smells. Seeking something familiar, he detects a musky scent: spicy and exotic. He follows his nose to its source.

"Hello, Harvey," Mrs. Fradette says. She's sitting on a chair with a napkin on her lap. She empties the crumbs on the floor for Harvey. This is enough of a reason for Harvey to stick close to her. "You're a good boy, aren't you? And you have your Maggie. You're so lucky."

Harvey doesn't understand the words Mrs. Fradette whispers, but he gives her another lick of approval because he realizes it is her smell Maggie comes home with.

"There you are!" Maggie says to Harvey. Then she looks at Mrs. Fradette. "My dad texted that he's running late."

Mrs. Fradette perks up. "We could finish our chat." Maggie's feet are light as she and Mrs. Fradette head back to the suite. They settle into the same spots as they had before, with Harvey lying at Maggie's feet.

"You didn't really give up on being a mechanic, did you?" Maggie wants to know.

Mrs. Fradette sighs. "Well, I had my return ticket for the Monday train back to Winnipeg. But it wasn't just the garage I was saying goodbye to."

"Peggy!" Maggie says.

Mrs. Fradette nods. "My little fawn had grown! Ronny couldn't believe she was as tame as she was. She came to my call and ate out of my hand. I think she'd have slept in my bed if I'd let her. Pépère had promised he'd let her stay in the yard and keep an eye on her, which put my mind at ease.

"The problem that was weighing on me was the garage and how to tell my dad I wanted to stay. The night before we were supposed to go, I lay in bed with my suitcase packed and my stomach in knots. I knew that if I got on that train without saying anything, I'd regret it."

Harvey feels Maggie tense. "What did you do?"

Mrs. Fradette sighs. "Nothing."

"Nothing?"

"I chickened out. I couldn't go through with it. The morning of our departure, Aunt Cecile, Uncle Joe, and their boys came to the house to see us off. Dad called for me to get in the car. My heart was heavy as he loaded our suitcases into the trunk and Yvonne climbed into my lap. Everything in me was crying to stay. Pépère got into the driver's seat of the Plymouth and put the key in the ignition. When he turned the key, the engine turned over, but the car didn't start.

"Dad checked his watch. There was only one train back to Winnipeg and it left promptly at ten in the morning every Monday. 'Hmm,' Pépère said. 'Strange.' It *was* strange because Pépère kept his car in pristine condition. It ran like a dream.

"'What do you think it is?' Dad asked.

"'Don't know,' Pépère said. He got out of the car and popped the hood so he could have a look. The rest of the family was still on the front porch watching all this. Michel and Yvonne were already wiggling around on Ronny's and my laps.

"We could hear Pépère and Dad talking. I kept waiting for Pépère to slam down the hood and the two of them to get back in the car. All of a sudden, I heard my name. Ronny and Mom looked at me. 'Dad's calling for you,' Ronny said.

"I slid Yvonne off my lap and opened the car door. Dad was seething beside Pépère. 'Your grandfather won't fix the car,' he said. I stood there, my eyes as big as saucers. 'He says you have to fix it.'

"I was too scared to move a muscle. What if I couldn't fix it? I looked at Pépère, but his face was stern as stone. Dad huffed and crossed his arms. By now, everyone on the porch had come to see what the holdup was and I had an audience, which didn't help.

"I took a few steps closer to the engine and did a quick survey. Things looked to be in order. All the connections were correct. Fluid levels good. I remembered the sound the engine had made. I'd heard that noise before and racked my brain to recall whose car it was and what the solution had been.

"That's when it came to me. The car had been a 1938 Dodge. 'I need tools,' I said.

"'Well, what are you waiting for?' Dad said, glancing at his watch. 'The train will be here soon!'

"Mom had insisted we wear traveling clothes and I felt ridiculous racing across the yard to the garage in my shiny church shoes and dress. She was going to have my hide if I got it dirty, so I grabbed a smock from a hook as well as the tools.

"I steeled myself as I began the repair and hoped I was right about what I thought needed to be fixed. We didn't have time to waste on a mistake. Behind me, I heard Dad snort with disbelief. After weeks of Pépère's teaching, I knew my way around an engine better than he did.

"'Start her up,' I said to Pépère.

"He got back into the car and I held my breath. The engine rumbled to life. There was clapping and wide-eyed surprise from my father. 'Hot dog!' yelled Ronny. He ran up to congratulate me. 'Pépère knew you'd be able to fix it,' he whispered in my ear. I let the hood of the car slam into place. Behind the steering wheel, Pépère winked at me."

"They'd planned it!" Maggie says.

"Yep! By the time we got to the station, I'd made my case to Dad. He'd stayed silent for the whole car ride. He was a careful man and fiercely protective of us. I didn't know it at the time, but it wasn't letting me work at the garage that was the hard part for him, it was leaving me behind.

"'She's got a knack for it. She's been a big help these last few weeks and she's a quick learner,' Pépère said as we pulled up to the train station.

"Dad still didn't say anything as we all piled out of the Plymouth and hauled our suitcases out of the trunk. The train pulled into the station and I knew we didn't have much time. If I was going to be allowed to stay, he needed to tell me before I boarded the train.

"My stomach was twisted up something awful. It felt like the course of my life depended on his answer."

Mrs. Fradette pauses. Maggie's hands are in tight fists as she waits for Mrs. Fradette to finish.

"'Your mom might need your help with the little ones so she can get the house in order,' Dad said.

"'Aunt Winnie will be a better help than I am,' I shot back. "'You've got an answer for everything, don't you?'

"Every part of me was begging *please*, but pushing it any further was going to get me in trouble. Finally, Dad looked at Pépère. 'She's really got a knack for fixing cars?' he asked.

"'Better than any boy I've worked with.' I was glad Alphonse wasn't around to hear that! I glowed at his words though.

"Dad took off his hat and ran a hand over his slicked-back hair. I took a breath. 'If your grandparents agree, you can stay on for the summer.'

"'I can stay?' I shouted. 'I can stay! Yahoo!' I threw my arms around his neck and hugged him, then did the same to Pépère.

"'Who ever heard of a girl so happy to be rid of her family?' Mom asked. She was smiling, but with tears in her eyes.

"'I will miss you,' I said. But I knew that garage was where I wanted to be."

"They really let you stay?" Maggie says.

Mrs. Fradette leans across to pat Maggie's hand. "They sure did. That was the beginning of everything for me. All thanks to the flood."

Harvey can't read Maggie's mind, but if he could, he would know that Maggie is in awe of Mrs. Fradette. As one of the few female mechanics of her time, Mrs. Fradette was a trailblazer.

Maggie is also thinking what an excellent essay this will make.

Chapter 48

Maggie

B y the time Maggie returns home, her excitement about the essay has fizzled. She made the mistake of checking her phone when her dad picked her up. Just like with the movie theater photo, Lexi has struck a blow meant to leave a mark. The picture is of her and Brianne with wide, openmouthed grins, at Tubby's. The hashtags read #BFF #TwoIsBetterThanThree.

When she steps inside the house, things get worse.

"I bumped into Lexi's mom," Maggie's mom says as she heats up her dinner. "She was buying snacks for their sleepover this weekend. She was surprised I didn't know about it."

Maggie's face falls. "I wasn't invited."

Her mom winces. "Did you have a fight?"

"I—I don't think so." But as the realization sinks in, Maggie's chin trembles. *Two is better than three*. "I don't know." What used to be clear to her has grown murky; her friendship, but also what she wants. She was used to going along with things, following Lexi's lead, but now...

"Maybe they texted while you were at Brayside and you missed it?" her mom suggests.

Maggie shakes her head. She knows there's not going to be a text. Maggie trudges upstairs to her room. She's too wrapped up in thinking about the sleepover she hasn't been invited to, that she doesn't know whether she even wants to be invited to, to hear the jingle of Harvey's tag as he follows her. When she gets to her room, she slips in and closes the door. Harvey is left in the hallway, staring at the door. Alone.

Chapter 49

Harvey

Inside Maggie's room, Harvey can hear whimpers, sometimes a sob. He paws at the door. He wants to be inside with his Maggie, licking her tears away and burrowing his head so they are nestled side by side.

"Harvey," Maggie's mom calls. "Do you need to go out?"

Not even a full bladder will pull Harvey away from Maggie's door. He sits, resolute, inches away from it. "The last thing I need is you having an accident," Maggie's mom mutters as she comes up the stairs and sees Harvey. She sweetens the deal by offering a treat. Harvey's ears rotate at the word. *Treat.* He leaves his post and flies down the stairs. Maggie's mom holds the treat out to him and then tosses it out the sliding doors. He races to retrieve it but is barely over the threshold when he freezes. Ears pricked, tail poker straight. Every hair bristles on his back. Harvey's nose quivers. The elusive scent! There is a rustle by the fence and Harvey glimpses a flash of tail disappearing under the shed. Finally, he will be able to meet whoever has been coming into his yard.

Harvey leaps across the deck and down the wooden stairs. He flies over shrubs and grass and comes to a stop in front of the shed and starts barking. Unlike the squirrels that make hasty exits as soon as he gets close, this creature stays put.

Harvey edges forward, ready to spring. From under the shed there is a hiss, a nasty, spitting noise that makes every muscle in Harvey's body go rigid. His instinct tells him something isn't right. Every nerve in Harvey's body is on high alert.

Deep from his belly comes a loud, warning bark. *Get away!* this bark says. *Go!*

But the raccoon has a warning too. It hisses again from the darkness, growling at Harvey. Its teeth and claws are ready for a fight.

Harvey moves closer. He knows he has to stand his ground. His bark turns vicious, as if he is the bloodthirsty creature. From inside the house, Maggie looks out her bedroom window.

Harvey can't let up. A staccato drumbeat of snarls and rough barks, the likes of which Maggie has never heard, explode out of him. If she didn't know her little Westie, she would be scared of him.

The raccoon realizes she is trapped. Her beady black eyes flash in the dark, looking for an escape. There is a sliver of space at the back of the shed where the gravel has sunk. She moves toward it, silently, to evade Harvey. She's a thief of the night, used to sneaking and skulking. She can get past this yappy dog.

But Harvey's hearing is keen. As is his sense of smell. The scent of fresh gravel as she unearths it and the rattle of rocks tumbling into the hole make him pause. Only for a second, but it's enough for him to know that his enemy is on the move.

One black claw, then another, appears at the back of the shed. This is his chance. He doesn't wait for the rest of her. He scurries under the shed with a savage bark, ready to attack.

"Harvey!" Maggie shrieks when she gets outside, breathless from racing down the stairs. She has seen him go under the shed and knows there must be something under there, but what? Her dad is beside her telling Maggie to stay back. Maggie ignores him and runs to the shed. "Harvey!" she shouts again over the barking. She's never heard him like this. He sounds like a wild, violent thing; like a guard dog meant to terrify.

Harvey registers Maggie's voice, but won't be deterred. He's a ratter. The raccoon is in his territory and the chase is on. He bares his teeth, muscles tense. He'd tear into the creature if that were in his nature, which it isn't.

But it is in the raccoon's.

The opening she'd hoped to squeeze through is too narrow. She is trapped again and now the dog is under the shed with her, snarling and barking. She realizes there is only one chance for freedom and that is attack. She turns to the dog, easily spotted even in the dark thanks to his shiny white coat, and lunges.

Her teeth sink into Harvey's back. They plunge deep and her claws hold his scrambling legs. A high-pitched yelp pierces the air as Harvey feels a sharp pain. His barking stops.

The raccoon could do more damage. She's injured Harvey. Badly. But raccoons are survivors, not fighters. She can see her escape route and takes it.

"Harvey!" Maggie is crying now, powerless to do anything from outside the shed. He won't come at her call. When she hears his yelp, she swears her heart skips a beat. She goes down on her knees to drag him out, but her dad pulls her back. He's grabbed a shovel and holds it, ready to swing.

"Stay back!"

"He's hurt!" Maggie screams again. Her heart is pounding when the raccoon slinks out. Her dad chases it with the shovel, but his threats are needless. The raccoon wants out of the yard. It hurries to the fence, climbs a post, and disappears into the night. Maggie stretches her arms as far under the shed as she can, but she can't feel Harvey. Her mom stands behind her with a flashlight. Maggie's dad drops the shovel and falls to his stomach, arms reaching out.

Harvey feels hands pawing him. He blinks at a beam of light, but he's too weak to move. "I've got him," Maggie's dad says.

Maggie is crying too hard to ask if he is alive. The sound of their fight still rings in her ears.

As gentle as Maggie's dad tries to be, yanking Harvey out of the hole is no easy task. Maggie stands by watching as a limp Harvey is dragged out from under the shed. He feels nothing but the beat of Maggie's heart as she holds him tightly.

Harvey shuts his eyes, breathing in her smell, and then goes still.

Chapter 50

Austin

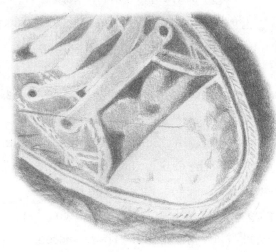

I get the message as soon as I arrive at Brayside on Friday. I haven't even taken off my backpack when Artie passes it to me. "Maggie called first thing this morning. This is her mom's cell. She said it was serious."

It has to be something about Harvey. Was he hit by a car? Lost again? A bunch of ideas run through my head, which makes the twenty seconds I wait for her to pick up seem even longer. "Austin?" she says.

"Yeah. It's me. Are you okay?"

"Yes. No. I mean, I am, but Harvey's not. We're at the animal clinic."

"What happened?"

Artie is watching my reaction and Mary Rose is there too. Their faces are pulled tight with worry.

"He got in a fight with a raccoon and got bit. He's hurt really bad." Maggie's voice cracks and she takes a shuddery breath. "They had to sedate him and he needed surgery."

"Is he going to be okay?"

"I don't know. The bite might have hurt his spine."

"Where are you?"

Maggie takes a breath. "Southside Animal Hospital." I grab a piece of paper off the desk and write down the name. "I'll see if my grandpa can take me. I'll call you back."

I hang up and tell Artie and Mary Rose what happened. "Oh, poor Harvey!" Mary Rose says. "Those raccoons! I just hate them."

"I need to see him." And the truth is I want to see Maggie too.

"Your grandpa's at the new building site," Artie says. "He'll be there all afternoon."

We look up Southside Animal Hospital. It's too far to walk to. My stomach is twisted in knots worrying about Maggie and Harvey. "I wish one of us could take you, but we have to stay here," Mary Rose says.

"I know," I say.

"There is someone else who has a car though." Artie and Mary Rose look at each other.

"I bet she'd do it too."

Artie prints out a map while Mary Rose heads down to the suite at the end of the hall.

Chapter 51

Maggie

Maggie's butt is numb from sitting in the waiting room for hours. Her dad stayed with her through the night and her mom has been with her for most of the day. She's left now to pick up her little sisters from day care. She wanted Maggie to go home for a while, but Maggie refused. She doesn't want Harvey to wake up alone.

Tired and stressed, the worst thoughts are running through her head.

The vet said the raccoon bite was dangerously close to Harvey's spine. Maggie caught the look that passed between her mom and the doctor. If Harvey's spine is damaged, he might not be able to walk. Maggie can't let herself think about what would happen if Harvey is paralyzed.

Maggie hasn't told Lexi or Brianne where she is. Now that she knows about the sleepover and has seen the #TwoIsBetterThanThree photo from Tubby's, she can't reach out.

To be honest, there is only one person Maggie wants to talk to.

Maggie shifts in the chair, trying to find a more comfortable position when the door to the clinic opens. All day she has seen people come and go with their pets. Dogs, mostly, but there have also been a few rabbits, cats, and birds. The two people who walk in don't have a pet with them and it takes Maggie a moment to realize why.

They aren't here for the vet. They're here for her.

"Margaret!" Mrs. Fradette strides toward her, outpacing Austin. "I heard! Your poor dog!"

"Hey," Austin says, frowning. "We wanted to see how you're doing."

Their genuine concern brings a new flood of tears to Maggie's eyes. "He's still in surgery."

She explains about the bite and that it went into Harvey's deep tissue, dangerously close to his spine, and the excruciating wait for the surgeon to do the operation. "I haven't seen him since we got here."

Mrs. Fradette sits down and takes Maggie's hand in hers. Mrs. Fradette is in a brightly patterned dress and carrying her ridiculously large black purse, which she keeps on her lap. "He's a tough dog. He'll make it," Mrs. Fradette says.

Austin sits on Maggie's other side. He doesn't hold her hand, but he does put his arm on the armrest, touching Maggie's. The small act comforts her.

"He wouldn't back down," Maggie says. "And I couldn't do anything to help. I've never heard him bark that way." All at once a new wave of despair takes over and Maggie struggles to hold back her tears. "What if he—"

Mrs. Fradette pats Maggie's knee. "I haven't told you what happened after Dad let me stay in Laurier, have I?"

Maggie wipes her tears and shakes her head, welcoming the distraction from worrying about Harvey.

Mrs. Fradette shifts her purse on her lap and begins speaking.

"Once Dad said I could stay in Laurier, it was decided I'd live with my grandparents. I wasn't thrilled about it; I would have preferred to stay at Aunt Cecile's. Even her eight boys were more enticing than Mémère. But Mom thought Mémère could use the help and I think she knew my grandmother was the only person who had a chance of keeping me in line.

"Her list of chores was as long as my arm and had to be completed before I was allowed to go to the garage. I fell into bed exhausted at the end of every day, but I knew I'd made the right choice. I was as happy as I'd ever been." Mrs. Fradette smiles at the memory. "I had Peggy too. She'd doubled in size about a month after we found her, but she still didn't want to leave our yard. It was as much her home as it was mine.

"Norm Lacroix continued to be a thorn in my side. Even though Pépère had told his father he should stay away from me, he kept turning up like a bad penny.

"Pépère came home grumbling one day after he caught Norm and a few of his friends smoking behind our garage. He sent them packing, but Norm never seemed deterred. He just kept coming back. Sometimes, he'd show up by himself, sidling up to where I was working and leaning against the car asking questions. I thought he was just being annoying, and I'd ignore him, but after a few weeks of this, it was Alphonse who figured it out. 'He likes you.'

"'Does not.'

"'Sure he does. Look at the way he's always hanging around.' Alphonse had become like a brother to me after all our weeks working in the garage. The competition that had existed when I first arrived had mellowed. We often ate our lunch together and talked about the latest radio shows. Alphonse loved cars and went through his dog-eared copy of auto magazines pointing out the cars he wanted to own one day.

"'He hangs around because he's Norm Lacroix, which is French for *irritating*.'

"But Alphonse shook his head. 'He's looking for your attention. Trust me.'

"The thought of Norm liking me turned my stomach. I didn't know why he would; I'd thrown rocks at him and chased him with a welding torch. When he came around, I didn't give him the time of day.

"'Josephine!' Pépère called. He had a car hoisted up on the lift and was welding its axle. It was a tricky one. He had on his welding goggles that made him look like a space invader. He passed me a wet sponge and told me to climb into the car. 'If you see any sparks, you need to put them out.' With all the chemicals in the garage, even one that smoldered could spell disaster.

"When Pépère was finished, he asked if I wanted to have a go. Of course, this wasn't my first time with a welding torch, but Pépère didn't mention it, and neither did I. He brought an old hubcap over and let me try welding the spokes back together. I put the goggles over my eyes. They were steamy and heavy. My hands were too small for the gloves and I was clumsy in them. I was concentrating on not dropping the torch and on the flame that shot out the end of it.

"Out of the corner of my eye, I saw Norm appear. 'Hey there, Josephine,' he called.

"At first, I pretended not to hear him. 'Hey there!' he called again. 'You're wearing goggles this time.' He gave me an oily grin. It was clear he wasn't going away unless I sent him away.

"I turned the flame off and pushed the goggles up onto my forehead. 'What do you want?'

"He shrugged and stuffed his hands in his pockets. 'There's a dance at the parish hall on Saturday. Did you know about it?'

"I'd seen posters. They were up all over. 'What about it?'

"'Wondered if you were going.'

"I almost dropped the welding torch. There I was, covered head to toe in soot and grease. 'To the dance?' I asked. 'No.'

"'Did you want to go?' he asked.

"'No.' I looked at him like he'd asked me to go to the moon. Norm's face flushed bright red and he turned away, embarrassed. That was when I realized he had been asking if I wanted to go with him.

"'What was that all about?' Alphonse asked from under the hood of a car.

"'Norm asked me to a dance,' I said, still confused by the whole exchange, 'but I said no.'

"Alphonse snorted. 'That took guts.'

"'To ask me?' With the welding torch in one hand, goggles over my eyes, and smudges of grease on the boys' coveralls I wore, I would have agreed that any boy who wanted to spend time with me was either brave or blind.

"'To say no.'

"'Pfft. Norm?' I still remembered how he had scampered away when I'd come at him and his friends with the welding torch.

"Alphonse shrugged. 'He's got a mean streak; all the Lacroix folk do. They think because they have money they're better than the rest of us. Watch your back is all I'm saying.'

"I didn't think any more on Alphonse's words. Norm didn't scare me. I was sure I could handle whatever he sent my way."

Mrs. Fradette pauses. Both Austin and Maggie are engrossed in her story. For the moment, the reason they are sitting in a vet clinic has been forgotten as they are drawn into her memories.

"I should have listened to Alphonse," Mrs. Fradette says. The tone of her voice has turned serious. "Mémère and I were home when a truck pulled up into the front driveway. A man got out. He wore a wide-brimmed hat and khaki-colored clothes.

"'Is this the Desroches residence?' he asked from the porch. "'Yes.'

"'Your parents home?'

"I explained that they were my grandparents and Mémère spoke only French. 'My grandfather is at his garage across the field.' Peggy picked that moment to bound into the front yard. She liked greeting new people. 'Don't worry,' I told him. 'That's Peggy. She's harmless.'

"The man raised an eyebrow. 'This is your deer?'

"I nodded right away, worried he'd mistake her for something wild. 'We rescued her and we've been raising her. She's tame.'

"The man's friendliness disappeared. 'You know it's illegal to keep wild animals on private property?'

"Mémère appeared behind me. She asked me in French

what the man wanted, but I didn't have an answer for her. 'There's been a report about an illegal animal on your property,' he said, and pulled a sheet of paper out of his shirt pocket. When he handed it to Mémère I saw the label across the top: CONSERVATION AND ANIMAL PROTECTION. 'This is a warning. I'm taking the deer with me today. If we find any other wild animals on the property, you'll be fined.'

"I stared at him for a moment, not understanding what was happening. Why was he taking Peggy? He went back to his truck and returned with a coil of rope.

"Peggy was so used to people, she didn't run when he came at her. She let him put the rope around her neck. He tightened it like a noose and my blood ran cold. 'Peggy!' I screamed.

"Mémère started ranting at the man in French. I screamed for Pépère and he came racing across the field from the garage. Peggy's eyes were wild and terrified at the man's roughness and our screams. She dug her feet in. I worried she'd break her neck twisting away from him. 'Stop it! You're hurting her!'

"'What's going on?' Pépère shouted. The man was sweating by the time he'd yanked Peggy up into the bed of his truck. The sides were wooden slats and I could see Peggy staring at me between the boards, terrified.

"'You can't keep wild animals.' The man slammed the back gate shut.

"Pépère sputtered. 'She's not wild. We've been raising her. She's as tame as the cat.'

"Peggy let loose a cry. A wail, really. It burned right into my ears. 'You can't do this!' I screamed. 'Where are you taking her?' I stormed up to the man and Pépère came after me. He knew it wasn't Peggy that was the wild thing to be worried about, it was me.

"But the man wouldn't answer us. 'She'll be set loose in a suitable environment,' was all he said as he climbed into the truck and slammed the door. 'Let this be a lesson to you. You can't tame wild animals.' I stamped my feet on the ground. What would Peggy do? After being with us for all these weeks, how would she survive?

"I fell against Pépère, sobbing. 'How'd he even know we had her?'

"Pépère let out a slow breath. 'Someone told him.' It wasn't until the dust cloud from the truck disappeared that I remembered Alphonse's warning about Norm."

Maggie and Austin sit with their mouths gaping.

Mrs. Fradette continues her story. "Nothing Pépère said made me feel better. I couldn't forgive myself for letting that man take Peggy, for not being able to protect her."

Maggie stiffens. Since she arrived with Harvey one thought has run through her head: *It's my fault.* She'd heard him scratching at her bedroom door and hadn't let him in. Regret sits heavily on Maggie's shoulders. If she hadn't been so wrapped up in Lexi's stupid text, Harvey wouldn't be here. He'd be cuddling on her bed with her. A new wave of tears is about to hit when Austin says, "It wasn't your fault."

For a moment, Maggie thinks he's reading her mind and his words are meant for her. But he's looking at Mrs. Fradette. "It was Norm's," he finishes.

"Was it?" Mrs. Fradette lets her question sit between them. "Of course," Austin says confidently. Maggie doesn't answer. She knows why Mrs. Fradette would blame herself. Before she got Harvey, her parents had told her over and over again that a dog was a "big responsibility" and now she finally understands what they meant.

It's not the walking and feeding and picking up poop. It's moments like these. Moments when she wishes she could turn back time and she can't. That is what responsibility is. It's knowing you might have to shoulder a burden you never asked to carry.

"What did you do?" Maggie asks, her voice thick.

"I needed to know if it was Norm."

Maggie nods. She would expect nothing less from Mrs. Fradette.

"I found him at his dad's office. Norm's face flushed bright pink the moment I walked in. His piggy eyes screwed up with guilt. He knew why I was there. 'Norm Lacroix! You good-for-nothing. They took away my deer!'

"Mr. Lacroix came out of the back room and shot daggers at me. 'What are you doing here?'

"'They took away my deer,' I said again.

"Lacroix laughed. 'Your deer? That's what all this is about?' I wanted to wipe that smug look off his face so badly." It's been over seventy years, but Mrs. Fradette balls her hands into fists as she talks. "'You're as crazy as your grandpa,' Lacroix muttered.

"'Pépère isn't crazy!' I was ready to storm across the room and do who knows what to him.

"'He's crazy for letting you work in that garage! Crazy for keeping a wild animal!' Lacroix said. Norm stood behind him and didn't say anything. His silence made me just as mad. He knew Peggy wasn't wild. He'd seen her in the field.

"I narrowed my eyes and pointed at Norm. 'If anything happens to her—' I started.

"Norm's father laughed. 'I don't think you should be making threats.' His meaning was clear.

"Angry tears stung my eyes. They were cruel, but I was powerless. For the first time in my life, I knew what it felt like to get beat.

"'You better run along,' Lacroix said. 'And don't come near my son again.'

"I stumbled out of their office, bleary-eyed with tears, and ran home. Peggy might have been wild, and me too maybe, but they were the beasts.

"Something in me changed after that. Losing Peggy haunted me. Where was she? How was she surviving? I'd taken her in, cared for her, but now she was defenseless. Maybe it would have been better if I'd followed Pépère's advice and left her in the ditch to let nature take its course.

"I started having nightmares about the day she was taken. As soon as I fell asleep, I saw Peggy's terrified eyes and heard her wails for help. In the dreams, Norm was holding me back, keeping me from going to her.

"At the garage, I was distracted. I tried to make sense of why that man had come to our house and it always came back to one thing: if I'd said yes to Norm's invitation to the dance, Peggy would still be here.

"When I said as much to Alphonse, he put down his wrench and looked at me. The bolts on the car he was working on were rusted and he'd been swearing a blue streak under his breath for the last hour. 'And what about when he asked you out again? You would have kept saying yes to something you didn't want to do?'

"'It would have saved Peggy,' I said miserably.

"'And cost you something else. There's no winning with people like them, because they have nothing to lose.'

"Pépère had said, 'A man like him needs to leave feeling like he's won.' And winning was all that mattered to Norm and his father. They were wrong to do what they did. They'd hurt an innocent animal, and caused me pain beyond anything I'd experienced before. But they'd never know any of that because you can only hurt if you love."

Mrs. Fradette squeezes Maggie's hand. "I know how scared you are right now. Loving something always comes with a risk; that's what makes it so special. Harvey knows you love him, Margaret. I promise."

Maggie's chin trembles at Mrs. Fradette's words. She didn't realize how much she needed to hear them until just now.

Chapter 52

Harvey

Harvey lies on a table on his stomach, silent and still. There is a tube in his mouth giving him oxygen and the drugs that will keep him unconscious until the surgery is over. An IV needle in one leg provides pain relief. He has a blue sheet covering his body. Only his head and the spot where the raccoon attacked are exposed.

A machine beeps in the room, tracking Harvey's heartbeat and blood pressure. The vet's assistant keeps an eye on it as she passes instruments to Dr. Parker, a specialist in canine spinal repair.

Her eyes flash to a number on the bottom of the screen. Harvey's temperature plummets. "Dr. Parker," she says, and gestures with her eyes to the screen. "He's going hypothermic."

She watches as the numbers steadily decrease. There is a flurry of activity as she and Dr. Parker jump into action. Harvey can't hear the commotion or the call for a heating device that will warm him up. He isn't aware that Dr. Parker picks up the pace of the surgery. Losing this Westie on the operating table is not an option. He's seen the girl in the hallway who refuses to leave even for a moment. She reminds him of his own daughter. He can't imagine going into the hallway and saying anything other than *The surgery was a success*.

"Stay with me, Harvey," he mutters, snipping a thread. "Someone out there needs you."

Harvey shouldn't be able to hear the doctor. He shouldn't be conscious of anything as he lies on the table. But from the black emptiness in which he floats, he feels a pull.

A tug.

His Maggie needs him. He can't let her down.

Chapter 53

Austin

Listening to Mrs. Fradette reminds me of sitting with Mr. Pickering. I get a flash of missing him, but it fades when Mrs. Fradette starts talking again.

"Pépère had been trying to pull me out of my slump by giving me more challenging tasks at the garage. I liked welding, the hiss of the flame and the way it magically healed broken things. I'd graduated from working on hubcaps to axle rods. When I brought something to Pépère, he'd inspect it, nod with approval, and ask if I'd checked for sparks.

"I always did, looking up every now and then to scan for them. This one day, about a month after Peggy had been taken, Pépère called quitting time. I pulled the goggles off my head and looked at the car driving by. It was a beautiful new Plymouth. Alphonse and I stopped and stared, wondering who the lucky owners were.

"It only took a second for me to see that in the passenger seat was none other than Norm Lacroix. I'd done my best to put him out of my mind, but seeing him sitting there so smug made my blood boil. Alphonse turned away and snorted with disgust. I stomped around the garage, tossing tools onto shelves, sure they'd driven past our garage to gloat.

"'Check for sparks?' Pépère asked as he pulled down the garage doors.

"I nodded, even though I knew I hadn't. All I could think about was how unfair it was that people like the Lacroix family got a new car. I stomped home ahead of Pépère and stuck to myself for the rest of the night, happy to wallow in missing Peggy and wishing bad thoughts on every member of the Lacroix family. The wish came true, but not in the way I expected.

"What happened next I only know because Pépère told me. He got woken in the night by Henri standing on his chest. It gave him such a fright because the cat had never done that before. He pushed Henri off and tried to go back to sleep, but Henri would have none of it. He persisted, meowing and using Pépère's arm as a scratching post until Pépère got out of bed. That's when he smelled it. Smoke.

"He ran to the window. 'Fire!' he yelled, loud enough to wake our house, and probably Aunt Cecile's. By that time, flames were licking at the roof of the garage. Pépère raced out of the house in his pajamas. Mémère followed behind with boots for him to put on. I wasn't far behind, and in my nightgown. 'Call the operator,' Pépère yelled to me. I ran back inside, my hands trembling as I dialed O. The nearest fire truck was in Ste. Rose and made up of volunteers who had to be roused from their beds. I knew that by the time it arrived, there'd be nothing of the garage left to save.

"But it wasn't the garage we were worried about; it was the house.

"The fire made the whole sky glow orange. It was as bright as daytime. Its heat scalded our skin even from where we were standing. Aunt Cecile, Uncle Joe, and the boys arrived with buckets filled with water from the stream. Pépère yelled at them to stop. Throwing water on burning gasoline would only spread the fire. 'Get back! It's too dangerous!'

"The words hadn't left his mouth before an explosion ripped through the back wall of the garage. Sparks and flames shot out. Nothing was going to put out that blaze. Pépère stared in shock. Mémère muttered prayers in French, her hand at her throat. Alphonse sobbed, watching the fire grow.

"Fear at what had started the fire crawled up my throat. Pépère had asked if I'd checked for sparks. I'd lied and said yes, but the truth was, I'd been preoccupied by Norm and his new car. A spark could have landed on a pile of rags and smoldered, finally catching and making its way to a can of motor oil, or maybe the welding cylinders, or the basin of gasoline we used for washing up. Had the blaze been my fault?

"As if in answer, there was another explosion and part of the roof fell with a crackling *thud*. We jumped back. Sparks flew, the wind carrying them toward the house. Alphonse and Uncle Joe ran to get a ladder and climbed onto the roof of my grandparents' house, stamping out any spark that landed. By the time we heard the fire truck's siren, the garage was gone, but the house was still standing.

"When dawn broke, we were soot covered and weak with shock. I didn't want to move, but Aunt Cecile dragged me away. 'There's nothing to be done now,' she said. I crawled back into bed, smelling of smoke and staining the sheets with my grimy skin. As tired as I was, I couldn't sleep. Every time I closed my eyes, I imagined a spark flying from my welding torch like demon spit.

"The next morning, I watched Pépère and the fire inspector survey the damage. The loss of the garage was a heavy blow to Pépère. They picked through the smoldering debris. The fire inspector shook his head at the destruction. What would Pépère do when he discovered I was the cause of the fire?

"We were all put to work salvaging what we could from the garage. The cars we'd been working on and the ones in the attached shed were just blackened shells. My guilt was compounded. I'd cost some families the only vehicle they had. Pépère was as hollowed out as the garage. His life had been reduced to a pile of rubble and my heart ached for him. The inspector had promised a report by Monday and as that day crept closer, my fear of what would be in the report grew.

"How could I stay? How could I look out at the empty lot where the garage had once been? Or see the lines etched in Pépère's face, knowing I'd caused them?

"Lying in bed on Sunday night, I tossed and turned. I couldn't stay and wait for the inspector to tell him what I already knew.

"I still had the unused portion of my return ticket to Winnipeg. The realization of what I had to do sat in my stomach like a rock. I didn't sleep a wink and snuck out before dawn with my few belongings stuffed into a suitcase. I'd left a note on my pillow thanking Mémère and Pépère for everything and confessing my guilt. There really weren't words to explain how sorry I was. When the garage had gone up in smoke, so had my dream of being a mechanic."

I look over at Maggie. She slumps in her chair. "Please tell me you didn't leave," she mumbles. With Harvey hurt, I don't think Maggie can handle a sad ending to Mrs. Fradette's story. But I know from Mr. Pickering that sometimes stories don't end the way you want them to.

"I went to the station," Mrs. Fradette says. "And sat on a bench waiting. Right on schedule, the train chugged into the station. My feet were leaden as I walked across the platform. Gripping the handle of my suitcase tighter, I willed myself not to turn around. The fire was my fault and letting go of my dream was the consequence. It was a hard lesson to learn at twelve."

"No," Maggie murmurs.

Mrs. Fradette pauses. She reaches over and covers Maggie's hand with her own. "It was time to board. I looked back once, saying goodbye to Laurier, and that was when I saw it."

"Saw what?" I whisper.

"A deer. It leaped over the tracks and stood watching me."

"Peggy!" Maggie says.

"I didn't know for sure," Mrs. Fradette continues. "She wasn't a fawn anymore. She was fully grown, but the way she looked at me, well—" Mrs. Fradette breaks off, her meaning clear. "*Could it be?* I wondered. I was holding up the line watching the deer. My heart hammered in my chest because if it was Peggy, I couldn't board the train without saying goodbye.

"'Ticket?' the station agent asked, holding out his hand. I hesitated. The woman behind me huffed with impatience. I held out the paper ticket, damp from my sweaty palm. He was about to take it when I snatched it back."

Maggie and I both let out a sigh of relief.

"I left my spot in line and walked across the platform, then jumped down to the gravel. I didn't want to scare her away, so I walked slowly, one hand outstretched. She was so much bigger than when she'd left me. Her coat was all brown now, with a white underbelly. She bent her head and took a few steps closer. 'Peggy?' I whispered. She didn't move, so I sat down on the ground, cross-legged, like I used to on the veranda. She took a few steps closer and sniffed the air. Then, slowly, she leaned forward and curled her front legs under her and sank down. She rested her head on my knee and I knew it was Peggy."

"She found you?" Maggie says.

Mrs. Fradette nods. "The train whistle blew and the conductor yelled, 'All aboard!', but I couldn't get up. I couldn't even move. It felt like a miracle that she'd found me when I needed her the most.

"The train chugged out of the station as Pépère came racing onto the platform yelling my name. 'Josephine!' he shouted, and slapped at a post when he realized the train had left and he was too late.

"I waited a breath, still scared of what he'd do, but knowing I'd missed my chance to leave. I was going to have to face the consequences, whatever they were. 'Pépère,' I said.

"He looked over and blinked like he couldn't believe his eyes. 'Josephine!' He jumped off the platform and came to me, stopping a few feet short, his face filled with wonder at the sight of me and the deer. 'It can't be.'

"'It is. It has to be. She found me.' I stroked the space between her eyes, down to her nose. She closed her eyes, content.

"Pépère looked at my suitcase. If he was at the station it meant he'd found my note. He knew why I was leaving.

"'You didn't cause the fire, Josephine.'

"I stared at him, sure I hadn't heard right. 'But the welding torch…I didn't check for sparks.'

"Pépère shook his head. 'It started outside, at the back. From a cigarette most likely.'

"A face flashed in my mind. 'Norm Lacroix!' I said.

"Pépère gave a reluctant nod. 'Maybe.'

"'He should go to jail!' That boy had caused nothing but trouble. He'd cost me Peggy, and his carelessness had cost Pépère everything!

"Pépère was resigned when he said, 'He probably won't. He's a Lacroix.' Which was French for 'Could buy his way out of punishment.'

"'It wasn't my fault,' I said with a sigh, not quite believing it. Of course, the truth about the cause of the fire didn't change the fact that the garage was gone.

"'We've got our work cut out for us rebuilding. I can't have you running away.'

"'I wasn't running—' I started, but the look on Pépère's face stopped the lie before it left my lips. 'I was worried you'd hate me,' I confessed.

"I realized how cowardly it sounded and hung my head in shame. Pépère lifted my chin, forcing me to meet his eyes. 'Anyone can handle an easy road. It's driving the rough ones that makes us who we are.'"

Mrs. Fradette gets quiet for a minute, lost in her memory.

"I've never forgotten that lesson. He was a wise man, my pépère." Her voice is soft when she continues. "We sat in the field by the station for a long time. I didn't want to get up because it would mean breaking the spell with Peggy, who'd fallen asleep with her head on my lap. I think it might have been the only moment of peace Pépère had had in days.

"Eventually, though, Peggy stood up. As gentle as she was, she was still a wild thing. She belonged to the forests and the fields, free. 'Bye, Peggy,' I whispered. In my heart, I thanked her for coming back, for saving me. Pépère and I watched as she walked toward the forest and leaped back across the tracks. In an instant she'd disappeared in the trees. That was the last time I saw her," Mrs. Fradette says.

When she's done, no one talks. Maggie lets out a long, shaky breath. I glance at Mrs. Fradette. She's still holding Maggie's hand. I'm so caught up in thinking about Peggy and Mrs. Fradette's story that I don't notice the vet until he clears his throat. "Maggie? I have news."

Chapter 54

Harvey

When Harvey opens his eyes, nothing is familiar. He doesn't like the smell of this place, wherever he is. Through bars, he can see the room is empty and his heart pounds. Where is his Maggie? Why does his body ache? The grogginess subsides and he raises his head to howl. If his Maggie is nearby, she'll answer.

He lies back down on his front paws and listens. There are voices and then the door opens. He catches a whiff of a familiar scent.

His Maggie.

She puts her face close to his, but the bars separate them. "Can I take him out?" she asks.

The answer is no, so she puts a finger through the bars. He licks it, and the taste of her is comforting. He gets a whiff of her tears, the worry and fear making them sharp. He doesn't care that he doesn't know this place. All that matters is that she is here.

"His recovery will take some time. He can't jump or run until the stitches dissolve. And, most importantly, no more battles with raccoons," Dr. Parker the vet says.

Maggie gives a half-hearted smile. "Hear that, Harvs? No more fights."

Harvey lies down again. He's so tired. As he closes his eyes, it's Maggie's face and the comfort of her scent that sends him to sleep.

Chapter 55

Maggie

The windows are open even though the October air has a chill to it. Mrs. Fradette holds the steering wheel of her Bel Air firmly. Without realizing it, she smiles as she pulls into traffic. A slow and careful driver, she hums to herself.

Maggie sits back on the red leather bench seat. Compared to her parents' cars, the front seat of the Bel Air feels like a couch. Nothing is automatic in this car. She had to manually crank the window open and she sees the effort Mrs. Fradette uses to turn the wheel. She stretches her legs in front of her and lets the breeze from the open window blow her hair across her cheeks. Mrs. Fradette's hair, of course, doesn't move.

It is a short drive to Tubby's and when Maggie gets out of the car, she notices a few people turn their heads. Mrs. Fradette pats the trunk as she walks to the curb, the way someone might pat the shoulder of an old friend. The chrome shines in the sunlight. "Glad you decided to keep it?" Maggie asks, although she knows the answer.

Maggie holds the door open for Mrs. Fradette. She stands in the doorway of the restaurant for a minute, taking it in. "It's just how I remember it!" she exclaims. Maggie believes it, with the fake wood paneling and red vinyl chairs. Black-and-white photos on the walls show old cars waiting for drive-in service from girls on roller skates. Others show young people sitting at booths with old-fashioned milkshake glasses; a few are even in St. Ambrose uniforms.

It has been a week since Harvey's tussle with the raccoon and he is healing well. Maggie puts him in a kennel when she leaves for school to make sure he doesn't hurt himself. He also isn't allowed to visit Brayside for a while, but Maggie gives the residents almost daily updates on his progress. She knows she came terrifyingly close to losing her little Westie.

Lexi and Brianne were concerned too when they heard. The last week has been fraught with weird friend tension; it isn't just the St. Ambrose kilt and knee socks that irritate Maggie these days. She keeps Lexi and Brianne at a cautious distance, still unsure where she stands with them. Without their constant presence, Maggie is discovering other girls who might be a better fit. For now, she is done with the prickly points of a triangle. Three was never an easy number anyway.

They find a booth by a window. Sitting across from Mrs. Fradette, Maggie feels shy all of a sudden. She invited Mrs. Fradette to Tubby's to say thank you for coming to the vet clinic. She and Austin showed up just when Maggie needed them the most.

"They haven't changed a thing," Mrs. Fradette says, staring around the restaurant in wonder. "I don't know if that's good or bad!"

Good, Maggie decides. Like the Bel Air.

"I was wondering about something," Maggie says. "Did Pépère rebuild the garage after the fire?"

"Oh yes. Insurance covered the loss. He built a bigger garage with three bays for repairs and a proper lift. I'd go up every summer to work with him." Mrs. Fradette smiles. Her purse is on her lap and she unsnaps the clasp and pulls out a photograph. It's worn and softened by time. In it, Mrs. Fradette's hair is piled high on her head. She is holding up a paper and beside her is an old man, his dark hair shot through with gray. His hand is on her shoulder and he is beaming with pride. "The day I became a mechanic, Pépère was there."

"So you did it. Even after the garage burned down," Maggie says.

"*Because* the garage burned down. But it wasn't easy. It was the 1950s. Men weren't used to having a woman in the garage with them. Every day, I had to prove I belonged there."

"You took the rough road." Maggie grins at Mrs. Fradette. Mrs. Fradette smiles back. "I sure did. And it made for a very interesting ride."

Maggie swells with pride for Mrs. Fradette. The other customers probably see an old lady with a black helmet of hair in a garish outfit, holding a too-big purse.

But Maggie wishes they could see what she is and has done. A trailblazer and a storyteller. A woman who was a wife and a mother. Someone who was young once, with dreams and challenges just like Maggie. And who was stubborn enough not to let them go.

Chapter 56

Maggie

Harvey's different since the fight with the raccoon. It's been three weeks, but Maggie can tell the wound still bothers him. He can't jump up on furniture, or go up the stairs. Instead, he sits at the bottom and whines, a reminder that he can't get up there without her help. They go for slower walks and even when a squirrel races in front of them, Harvey doesn't try to tear after it.

Will he ever be back to normal? she wonders.

In some ways, the new Harvey fits the new Maggie. She doesn't mind that he's more cautious. She knows how close she came to losing him. But today is a day for celebration. Dr. Parker has cleared Harvey for a visit to Brayside. It will be the first time since Austin's grandpa's work-iversary and the old people are anxious to see him.

Lexi and Brianne, so concerned after Maggie told them about the raccoon attack, have cooled toward Maggie now that Harvey's getting back to normal. Lexi's attitude is ramping up and Maggie sees her hungry glances at the table of popular girls while they eat in the cafeteria. She wishes Lexi would just go already and stop pretending she's where she wants to be.

Maggie knows who her real friends are anyway.

She never expected to find them at Brayside when she signed up for volunteer hours, but that's what happened. She's not sure she could have made it through Harvey's surgery and recovery without Austin. Of everyone in her life, he understood how much Harvey meant to her, because, she suspects, he means as much to Austin. Which is why she is so excited about what she is about to do.

Austin's grandpa is waiting on the sidewalk when Maggie, her mom, and Harvey pull up to the curb in front of the animal shelter. Austin's grandpa and Maggie's mom shake hands warmly. "Call me Phillip," he says.

All of them peer through the front window into the plexiglass cage inside. They are looking at a puppy with floppy brown ears too big for her head. There is a spot of brown on her back and another around each eye. She snoozes beside another dog in a bed of shredded newspaper, oblivious to the three people staring at her from the sidewalk.

"She's so much bigger!" Maggie says, remembering the newborn who fit in Austin's hand. "She looks like a real dog."

"What changed your daughter's mind?" Maggie's mom asks. "Maggie said she didn't want a dog."

Phillip smiles. His eyes are twinkly when he looks at Maggie. "It was Maggie."

Maggie's mom is taken aback. Lately, Maggie's maturity has been surprising her. There are glimpses of the person her child is becoming. "You didn't tell me that," she says, turning to Maggie. "What did you do?"

Maggie is happy to answer. "I made an attack plan. I thought of all her arguments and found a way around each of them." *Just like Mrs. Fradette would have done*, Maggie thinks.

Beside her, Phillip chuckles. "Austin's mom didn't stand a chance."

"First, there was what to do when Austin was at school. That was easy because Phillip's new building is closer to the apartment. He agreed to go over at lunch to let her out. Second was the dog's size. Big dogs aren't allowed at Austin's apartment, but the shelter thinks she's part Jack Russell and will be about Harvey's size. But the best part"—Maggie pauses here to let the last part of her plan stand out—"the best part is that everyone at Brayside contributed to the cost of the adoption and vet bills. We even had enough left over for a gift card to a pet store, for food."

Maggie's pride fills her with a warm glow. It feels like things have come full circle from last year when she found Harvey. Only this time instead of taking a dog from Austin, she is bringing him one.

Chapter 57

Harvey

When Harvey jumps out of Maggie's mom's SUV, he feels a twinge of pain. The fight with the racoon is a fuzzy memory now, as are the surgery and the weeks of recovery, but still there is that reminder that he isn't exactly as he used to be.

On the sidewalk, Harvey is drawn to a corner of the building. It is covered with so many smells that Harvey could sniff all day and not catch all of them. Maggie pauses so Harvey can add his scent. Beside her, Phillip chuckles. "Good job, Harvey."

Harvey doesn't know where they are or why, but listening to Maggie's quick-talking enthusiasm tells him it must be a good place. "Come on, Harvey," Maggie says, and goes through the door Phillip opens for them.

Harvey is almost all the way in when he takes a cautious sniff. Barks echo off walls; some are warnings and some are greetings, but Harvey is not concerned. He's with his Maggie.

"Harvey, look!" Maggie squeals, distracting him. The pitch of her voice is enough to get Harvey excited. But then he catches a whiff of a familiar odor. He digs deep into his catalog. Maggie is handed a wriggling thing and crouches down so it is nose to nose with Harvey.

She has grown, but Harvey would know the puppy anywhere. One ear flops and her legs squirm, eager to be free. This pup wants to run and jump and play. Harvey gives it a sniff and then a nuzzle. "Do you like her, Harvey?" Maggie asks.

Harvey is curious. He sniffs again. The barking dogs around him are forgotten. Harvey is still young himself, only four years old, but being around this tiny pup shows him that she has a lot to learn. It is instinct that tells him he is the one who will teach her.

The shelter is close enough to Brayside that they could walk, but instead Maggie, Phillip, and Harvey pile into Maggie's mom's SUV. Phillip sits in the front and on his lap is the kennel. It is a hand-me-down from Harvey, too small for him now. Inside the kennel, on a fleece blanket, the puppy whimpers.

Harvey knows she is scared. He would like to lie beside her, or perhaps lick her face. Either way, he would reassure her that she is safe. She will be cared for and she will be loved.

Chapter 58

Austin

Maggie warned me that she'd be late today. First, she had to take Harvey to the vet, but if he checked out okay, he'd come with her for a visit. I see her mom's SUV pull up in front of Brayside. Maggie gets out and opens the back-seat door for Harvey. He jumps down with more care than he used to, and trots toward the sliding doors. He doesn't need to wait for her. He always knows his way into Brayside.

I bend down and he runs right into my arms, raising his head to lick my chin. "How are you doing, Harvey?" I say. He still has a little bald patch where the stitches were, but in every other way, he looks normal.

Mary Rose comes around the front desk. "Are you happy to be back? Are you, Harvey?" she says in a singsong voice, which makes Harvey's tail wag faster.

"Yep! The vet gave him a thumbs-up," Maggie says. "Just no more fights with raccoons."

Harvey's sitting between us with his ears pricked like he knows we're talking about him. His white beard is especially scruffy today, sticking out all over the place like he's a dog version of Albert Einstein. "I never would have thought Harvey would be the fighting kind," Mary Rose says.

Maggie laughs. "Me neither!"

Lately, Maggie laughs a lot and I wonder if it's because of Mrs. Fradette. It's funny how old people rub off on you. She's becoming like one of Mrs. Fradette's outfits, brighter and bolder. I'm not worried about Maggie using up her twenty volunteer hours anymore. She's here for the long haul. "You're just in time for the sing-along," Mary Rose says to Maggie with a wink.

"Another sing-along," I grumble. I thought we were done with those now that Grandpa's job is safe.

"Oh, come on! All the old people want to see Harvey anyway." This was true. They'd been waiting all day to see if he'd show up. Funny how a little dog can bring such excitement to a place.

The games room is packed. All the usuals are there, but I'm surprised that Artie came on his day off. Louise is there too, pushing Mrs. Gustafson in a wheelchair. It's the first time I've seen Mrs. Gustafson out of her room in weeks. Maggie's face splits into a grin when she sees the room full of people. Harvey trots beside her and no one makes as big a deal about him as I thought they would. I mean, aren't they all here for him?

Maggie nods at Mrs. O'Brien and she comes up to me. Her eyes are shining. "Austin," she says, and looks behind me.

I turn to the door and see my mom. *What the heck?* "Mom? What are you—"

Grandpa is there too, but it's Mom I'm looking at because she's holding something in her arms. It's a puppy.

I stare at both of them for a minute because I don't believe it. "Austin," Mom says, and holds the dog out to me. For a second, I don't move. I've dreamed of this moment for so long. Grandpa and Mom are both waiting for me to do something. So are all the old people, and Maggie and Louise and Mary Rose and Artie.

"Go on," Grandpa says. "She's yours."

My hands tremble when I reach out and take her. It's the puppy Harvey found in the alley. The one I brought to the shelter and thought I'd never see again.

"Is she really mine?" I ask, because I still can't believe it. I'm sort of crying and laughing at the same time. Her fur is silky soft, and when I hug her to my chest she sticks out her pink tongue and covers my neck with kisses, even though she doesn't know me. Or maybe…maybe she does.

"But you said no dogs," I say to Mom.

Mom laughs. She's tearing up too. "I know, but Maggie is very convincing."

Maggie. She's standing with Mrs. O'Brien and Harvey is at her feet. "It wasn't just me," she says. "Everyone helped. They all put money in."

"If anyone ever deserved to have a dog, it's you," Miss Lin says. Mr. Santos, the Kowalskis, Mrs. Gelman, and Mr. Singh all nod.

"What are you going to call her?" Maggie asks.

The only name I could call her. It's been on my mind since the day I found her. It's a name that belongs to a strong spirit, a fighter. And I know Mr. Pickering would approve.

"Bertie," I say.

Chapter 59

Maggie

The cafeteria is almost full when Maggie arrives. She pauses at the entrance and sees Brianne and Lexi at their usual table. They have been joined by two other girls who are also in Student Leadership. There is an empty chair, which might have been saved for Maggie, or maybe it's just coincidence. The four girls are leaning in, whispering. Suddenly, they burst into laughter and get curious looks from students at nearby tables. Maggie's stomach twists. *If three was a bad number, five will be worse.*

Maggie scans the cafeteria looking for options. Across the room, she sees Sooyeon, a girl from her homeroom. Sooyeon is shy in class, but quick to smile. She was the only other student to enter the essay contest, which makes Maggie think they might have a few things in common.

Sitting with Sooyeon instead of Lexi and Brianne would be out of character for Maggie and would raise some eyebrows. Considering how precarious their friendship has been lately, Maggie's not sure she wants to risk it. But she's also not sure she can sit through another lunch hour pretending to be someone she's not.

Brianne spots her hesitating at the entrance. Maggie has to make a choice. She can't stand there all lunch hour. She glances once more at the empty seat beside Sooyeon, then back at Lexi and Brianne. With sudden clarity, she knows where she wants to sit and starts walking past Lexi and Brianne's table.

"Is it okay if I sit here?" Maggie asks. Sooyeon looks up from her sketchbook and smiles.

As Maggie pulls the chair away from the table, she looks up. Brianne and Lexi are watching her. She holds their gaze for a moment, then waves. It's a small, friendly gesture, meant to ensure there won't be hard feelings, or a flurry of text messages. After years of knowing the girls, she doesn't want to break the friendship, just stretch it a little.

Lexi raises her eyebrows and turns to Brianne. To Maggie's surprise, Brianne ignores Lexi and grins back at her instead. It's not a tug-of-war, but Maggie feels like she might have gained a bit of ground just by being herself.

Chapter 60

Harvey

When the door to the suite opens, Harvey is assaulted by the familiar musky smell. It's a Saturday and Maggie has brought him for a visit.

But they're not alone.

"Margaret! Austin! Bertie! And Harvey!" At his name, Harvey takes a step closer and is rewarded with a pat on the head. Bertie scampers into the room with excited puppy hops. Austin follows, trying to keep up.

"I have a surprise for you, Mrs. Fradette," Maggie says. Harvey heard all about the surprise on the way to Brayside. Maggie has talked of nothing else since her teacher gave her the good news yesterday. Harvey looks on as she hands the old lady a sheet of paper. "My history essay won second place!"

Mrs. Fradette opens her arms and hugs Maggie. "You clever girl! I knew you could do it!"

"Do you want to read it?" Maggie asks.

"You read it to me," Mrs. Fradette says, sitting down in her chair.

Maggie sits on the couch and Harvey jumps up to join her. Austin is not far away, holding Bertie on his lap. Harvey lies down and rests his head on his front paws, a lesson in good behavior for Bertie.

Maggie clears her throat. "'Oil and Water: The Story of Josephine Fradette' by Margaret O'Neil." Maggie sneaks a peek at Mrs. Fradette and grins. "'Mrs. Fradette was a pioneer for women in the field of auto mechanics. And it all started because of the Red River flood of 1950.'"

As Maggie reads her essay, Harvey sighs. This couch fits just right. He's surrounded by his people: his Maggie and his Austin, and little Bertie, who has a lot to learn. Harvey closes his eyes, content, and drifts off to the sound of Maggie's voice telling a story of perseverance and courage. Two things that Harvey knows a lot about.

Acknowledgments

My first thanks is to Wayne Pickering. As our family historian, he willingly shares his research with me and provided the seeds that blossomed into the characters in Mrs. Fradette's stories. *Harvey Holds His Own* is very loosely based on my maternal grandma's family history. I've borrowed real names and locations. I thought of my grandma, Marie Pickering, a lot as I wrote this story. I'm so grateful for the time I had with her as a child.

A very special thank you to Arlene Nelson, who passed away before this book was finished. Her stories about 'Bambi,' the deer she found and cared for, were the inspiration for Mrs. Fradette and Peggy.

My next round of thanks goes to the Pajama Press team: To Ann Featherstone for being a superb editor. To Erin Alladin, Lorena Gonzalez Guillen, and Laura Bowman who edit, design, promote, and ensure the book reaches its full potential. Special thanks to Erin who came up with the title! Thank you to Rebecca Bender for another brilliant cover and to Chandra Wohleber for her finely tuned copyediting skills.

There are others who have helped me with this book: Cindy Kochanski who read and commented on an early draft; Jeanne Brault who unknowingly inspired the character of Mrs. Fradette (she was Canada's first certified female mechanic); and Richard Jones of the website Old Classic Car for helping me with research.

It might come as a surprise to you that Harvey's illustrator Tara Anderson and I have never met. It amazes me that she is able to bring the Harvey in my head to life in her drawings. The book is so much better because of your talent, Tara!

Finally, thank you to Gail Winskill who is a champion to Harvey and to me. I am so lucky to have you in my corner.

Colleen and *Rosie*

An author and junior high school teacher, *Colleen Nelson* earned her Bachelor of Education from the University of Manitoba in her hometown of Winnipeg. Her previous novels include the critically acclaimed *Harvey Comes Home*; *Sadia*, winner of the 2019 Ruth and Sylvia Schwartz Award; and *Blood Brothers*, selected as the 2018 McNally Robinson Book of the Year for Young People. Colleen writes daily in between appearances at hockey rinks and soccer fields in support of her two sports-loving sons. Recently the family has welcomed a new member: Rosie the Westie, who has inspired many of Harvey's antics, including chasing squirrels and chewing shoes.

Tara with her childhood dog *Buffy*

A folk artist and award-winning illustrator who trained at the Ontario College of Art and Design, *Tara Anderson* is known for her lively and humorous illustrations of animals. Her books include the illustrated novels *Harvey Comes Home* and *Sapphire the Great and the Meaning of Life*, the Halloween picture book *Pumpkin Orange, Pumpkin Round*, and the award-winning *Nat the Cat Can Sleep Like That*, among others. Tara shares a farmhouse in Tweed, Ontario, with her husband, her young daughter, and several cats.